Four Little Gems

Four Little Gems

— David Grieve —

ISBN 978-0-9565296-0-2

Cover design by Clare Brayshaw

Prepared by:

York Publishing Services Ltd
64 Hallfield Road
Layerthorpe
York YO31 7ZQ
Tel: 01904 431213

Website: www.yps-publishing.co.uk

Contents

The following short story is a combination of fact and fiction. Some parts of the story are drawn from events that occurred during my schooldays. I hope you enjoy reading the tale as much as I have enjoyed writing it.

D A Grieve

Pushing Back

It was early December 1953, I was fourteen years old. I was standing outside the Headmasters office. My day had started badly, very badly. The head was in the habit of keeping the boy that was to be punished waiting. The long wait was part of the punishment. It was not yet 10am; whilst I waited, I thought over the events of that morning. The events that brought me to the predicament I was in.

Yet another cold, grey Monday morning had arrived. It felt to me as though Monday had impatiently shoved Saturday and Sunday out of the way and arrived early. I felt cheated. I was lying awake in my rickety, old, iron framed bed with a heap of Army surplus blankets pulled up around my ears. I was curled up in a tight foetal ball. Only the top of my head was exposed. A tiny opening allowed me to peer out at the gloomy morning. It was icy cold in my tiny box-like bedroom.

As I lay psyching myself up to get up, I heard the brass flap of the letterbox clatter noisily as my Father opened the front door. The door was sticky due to an overdose of cheap, council paint. Father bellowed at me. 'COME ON BOY, GET OUT OF THAT BED!' He then slammed the door behind him and made his was to work.

After a short while, I ventured exposing the whole of my head to the chilly air. Half a second later it was back in my warm cocoon. 'Sod that,' I murmured. While lying in the warmth I was tense and expectant; a few more minutes passed before Mother screeched up at me. 'COME ON DAVID, GET OUT OF THAT BLOODY BED AND DON'T FORGET TO HAVE A BLOODY WASH!' Even though I was expecting it, I still jumped at the sound of that voice. I didn't have time to give a lying reply such as; I'm already up Mum, as she was already out the front door and on her way to work. She also slammed it behind her.

I was more than a little reluctant to emerge from my cosy nest. However, strictly enforced parental rule dictated that I had to make the effort. In any case my older sister, who was already up, would inform Mother of any further tardiness of mine. So, I began my usual daft routine of slowly counting down from twenty to zero. The idea being that as soon I got down to zero I would jump out of bed. I must have counted down at least ten times before my feeble willpower got me motivated. However, I didn't exactly *jump* out of bed; I got out a bit at a time. First one leg, then an arm, a short pause. Then the rest of me would slowly and reluctantly emerge from the sanctity of my rough, military blankets.

I stood shivering in my underwear as I thought through the task of getting dressed. 'Socks first,' I muttered and began searching in the grey gloom of my bedroom. Switching the light on was not an option, the light bulb had long since blown. One wouldn't have thought that a pair of socks could be so elusive. During the hunt I came across my trousers so I abandoned the search for the socks and pulled on the long, grey flannels. As it happened, I found the socks in the back pocket of the trousers. I found my shirt and pullover folded up in a neat bundle on top of my shoes which were on the floor in their usual corner.

Once dressed, I sat on my bed contemplating getting washed. It was at that moment that I got the strange feeling that my day was not going to go well. I sighed deeply and looked around at my dismal bedroom. The walls were covered with faded and torn, flowery wallpaper. Faded flowery curtains hung unevenly on stretched, slack wires in front of rarely cleaned and rarely opened windows. There was a narrow, ceiling high, junk filled wardrobe built into the wall at the foot end of the bed, the door of which was festooned with stab wounds and dart holes. The well worn and cracked lino floor covering had holes in it through which I could see the newspaper underlay. I looked up at the cracked, flaking ceiling, sighed another deep sigh, stood up and made my way to the bathroom and toilet.

Moments later I was in the bathroom whereupon another search ensued. The icy cold was having its usual effect. I had difficulty finding my penis. After fumbling about for a minute or so, I ended up having to drop my trousers and pants. My penis had shrunk to such a degree that it resembled a small pink currant. As for my testicals, they seemed to have disappeared altogether! All the same,

3

I did manage a few short squirts and a passably loud fart; the bathroom was beginning to cloud up as a result of my breath being converted into mist in the extreme cold, so I decided that a quick wipe round with my dampened face flannel would suffice as far as washing was concerned. After combing my unruly, curly hair with wet fingers, I went down stairs to the kitchen for breakfast.

My sister, the lovely Margaret, who was four years my senior was sitting at the kitchen table. To say the least, Margaret was not a morning person bless her. She was attired in a rather *chic,* yellow, candlewick dressing gown. She was staring open-mouthed at the narrow strip of wall between the ceiling and the top of the net curtained window. On the table in front of her was a half eaten bowl of porridge oats. Grasped firmly in her right hand was a table spoon. The manner in which she held the spoon could, in any other circumstance, be construed as intimidating. In her left hand she held a cup of tea which was tilting precariously. The contents were a fraction away from being spilled onto the pink, gingham patterned, plastic table covering.

I tried to imagine what was going on inside her beautiful, dark, wavy-haired head. Not much, I thought cruelly. I wondered if she could see right through that strip of wall and was observing the aircraft flying too and from London Airport and wishing she was a passenger or crew member. For a moment I joined her in her fantasy; Margaret would snap out of her dream soon and would not be in the best of moods.

I looked around the small, cluttered kitchen. It seemed as if everything bar the floor, walls, gas cooker and sink was painted with layer upon layer of dull, green paint. On the wall opposite the doorway there was a two tiered set of double door cupboards below which was a distressed looking sideboard. I went to the cupboards to get a breakfast bowl. Heaven only knows how those cupboards remained fixed to the wall. There must have been at least a half hundred weight of all manner of crockery crammed into them. One would be hard pressed to find a single piece that wasn't cracked or chipped. Also, there were about eight different patterns and shapes to them, none of which comprised a full service; I managed to find a bowl that was in reasonable nick. I went to the table and plonked it down noisily. I glanced across at my sister. There was no reaction. I went back over and pulled open the cutlery draw in the sideboard to get a spoon. I fished out a table spoon from amongst the assorted cutlery that had accumulated over time. Scrap mettle would be a good description of most of the contents of the cutlery draw. I slammed the draw shut. Margaret didn't flinch.

There was a pan of porridge on the cooker. The gas ring beneath the pan wasn't lit. However, the one next to it was so the porridge wasn't quite cold. I turned off the gas and hefted the pan over to the table. I banged it down and glanced at Margaret; still no reaction. I sighed deeply and then set about digging out the off-grey stodge that lay challengingly at the bottom of the pan. I dug my spoon into the goo and drove it down until it hit mettle. Then, like a plough, I pushed the spoon across the full diameter of the pan. The edges of the furrow gave no indication of collapsing inwards. I levered the spoon upwards, taking care not to bend it. The porridge emitted a slurping, sucking sound. 'Stand by!' I said loudly; as the stodge gradually gave way I had visions of the spoon jerking upwards and a large lump of porridge being catapulted into the air and I would have to deploy my bowl in order to catch the air-born lump. Sadly though, this was not the case. The porridge submitted and I dumped the lump into my bowl. 'Gotcha!' I said; 'Silly sod,' said Margaret evenly. She had finally come too.

I greeted her with false joviality. 'Good morning Margaret.'

'That's your opinion daft arse.' She replied without a trace of joviality.

With her eyes blinking rapidly, she stared around the kitchen. It was as if she had never set eyes on the room before. She then sighed a deep sigh of resignation. It was time for her to make a move and get ready for work! She got slowly to her feet. Once she was fully upright she rested. After resting, she stretched her arms high and wide and yawned a gaping yawn after which, she had another rest.

'It's your turn to wash up you know.' I stated this with a smug grin on my face. Margaret threw a withering glare at me as she made her way out of the kitchen.

My false grin disappeared. It was time to eat breakfast. I did my best to empty my bowl. It was a valiant attempt but a vain attempt. I didn't manage it. Using Margaret's cup, I poured myself some tea, there was just enough in the big, brown pot. I sniffed the top of the near empty milk bottle. 'Mmm, not quite rancid,' I muttered softly and poured some into the strong, stewed tea. I then chipped out some tea-stained sugar from the cast-glass sugar bowl. I tipped the mined sugar into the tea and gave it a stir with my index finger. It tasted good.

Whilst preparing my cuppa I listened to Margaret getting herself ready. I wasn't eavesdropping, it was unavoidable. There was a lull of silence after she had reached the top of the stairs; I lost count of the amount of times she thumped back and forth from bathroom to bedroom. I reckoned that the amount of water Margaret used per morning would be enough to irrigate Q gardens. There would be a short interval of quiet before she fired up her hair-dryer. The noise of that beast put me in mind of a low flying single prop, light aircraft. It was a monster of a hair-dryer. In my minds eye, I could see the technicians at Battersea Power Station running around like blue-arsed flies throwing switches of all kinds in order to compensate for the drain on the national grid.

I smiled as I recalled the day when sis first got the hair-dryer. It was a gift on her fifteenth birthday. As soon as she'd ripped the wrapping off she ran upstairs and washed her hair. Ignoring the instructions completely, the silly mare plugged in and began drying. Needless to say, disaster ensued; I reckon Margaret was the first white, teenage girl to sport an Afro hairdo. The poor cow came running down stairs with tears streaming down her glowing red cheeks and I swear to this day, I saw wisps of smoke rising from the top of her woolly head. At the sight of the poor girl looking like that I very nearly collapsed with laughter. My father tried to slap my face straight, but he failed to beat the giggles out of me.

After taking a few more sips of my tea I decided it was my turn to make a move. At the same time, the hair dryer ceased its terrible racket. It was my turn to sigh a sigh of resignation. 'If ya gotta go, ya gotta go,' I uttered softly. I felt a pang of dread as a thought of school entered my head. I despised that damned school; For a few moments I stood gazing about the drab little kitchen of my home. Number 28 Holly House.

Holly house was built in the early nineteen thirties. It was an oblong, red bricked building. It consisted of two stories. There were thirty two maisonettes in all. My home was on the top story at the head of one of two stairways. A long, concrete balcony gave access to the maisonettes on the upper story. All the front doors were painted olive green and all the metal, French style window frames were painted a miserable cream colour and were dappled with patches of rust. There was a small balcony at the rear of each home on the top floor. They were all painted dull cream. My home was much the same as most working class homes of the day. Sparsely furnished. Cold in winter and uncomfortably warm in the summer. The living room was the least used room in the house. It had to be kept clean and tidy in case somebody important came to the house. Like the Doctor for instance.

My keen sense of hearing picked up the faint click of the front door latch as my crafty, underhanded sister closed the door quietly behind her. That sound was followed by the clack, clack, clacking of her high heeled shoes on the concrete balcony outside. I rushed to the window and squinted through the dingy net curtain; it was too late for me to do anything. The racket of her ankle-snappers clattering down the stairwell was already fading. Enraged at being lumbered with the washing up again, I shouted at the top of my voice 'YOU ROTTEN, HORRIBLE COW!' Unfortunately, at precisely that moment, Mrs Trimble from next door was passing the kitchen window! She almost jumped out of her skin! 'Oh shit!' I whispered hoarsely. Although I couldn't see her face clearly, I knew the hatchet faced, tyrant of a Woman was glowering at me. Every time I encountered Mrs

Trimble, she would look at me as though I was something that had just dropped out of a horses arse; Of course Mrs Trimble would be duty bound to inform my Mother that I had called her a rotten, horrible cow; The rotten, horrible cow!

My Mother would be no less duty bound to admonish me for the misdemeanour. She would give me her usual lecture on responsibility, morals and the loutishness of being disrespectful to my elders. Then, without warning and with practiced speed and accuracy she would clout me round the ear. I have to give the great Lady her due though; she always alternated between the ear that was to be clouted.

Well there I was standing in the shabby little kitchen of number 28. I felt miserable and extremely angry. Margaret had pulled a fast one. Not for the first time had she got one over on me. She knew well the dire consequences of my not clearing up the breakfast stuff. As always, she would be found to be blameless. I would be the one made to suffer. Needless to say, the pots and crocks took a bit of a battering. After a struggle that included a lot of mumbled obscenities, the gooey, sticky, cold porridge succumbed to my tenacity as a washer-up; with the awful chores out of the way, I donned my jacket and slammed out of the house. I was in a foul mood.

I shivered in the cold, damp air outside. The moisture of my breath swirled about my head. I looked along the length of the dull, cream balcony that fronted the upper floor of the building. There was no sign of Smelly Lenny, a neighbour and school friend. He was rarely at school due to his Mother being an alcoholic. His father had been killed in the war; The foul stink of the jammed open dust

9

chute at the side of the stair well assaulted my nostrils. I looked over the balcony. Below and opposite was a row of dilapidated coal sheds, the doors of which were painted, you've guessed it, green. To the right of those stood two of the five communal air raid shelters that were situated around Holly House. The grass covered, concrete structures had long since been bricked up. Between the two shelters there was a gravely area upon which there were three rows of washing poles. On one of the lines there hung motionless a lone garment. It was a pair of huge, greyish-white y-fronts. I looked up and over the long, high wall behind the sheds and the shelters. Overlooking all was a massive, grey-bricked Church building. It blended well with the leaden, grey sky.

I turned from the less than invigorating view, shivered, thrust my hands deep into my pockets and descended the gloomy staircase. A total of twenty two steps with a landing halfway down. I walked the length of the building to the dangerously cracked and crumbling path that led on to the gateless gateway set in the middle of a long, low, red-brick wall. At the gateway I glanced back at the plain, red, green and cream block of maisonettes. It wasn't much, but it was home.

My half mile journey to school was uneventful. I never stopped to fool around at any of the places I would normally stop at. My Sisters trickery had put me off of silly games. So, I kept my head down and walked on oblivious to the noise and stink of traffic and the throng of people going to and from their place of work. I heard my pal John Bacon calling to me to hang on and wait for him. I ignored him and hurried on. My mood was not improving. The thought that Margaret had fooled me again rankled still further. Not forgetting of course, it was Monday and I was almost at the school gates.

The tall, ornate, wrought iron gates marking the entrance to Brenton Secondary School for boys were locked open. I would have liked them to have been locked shut. Welded shut would have been better still. The long, stony path from the gate to the playground was lined on either side by high, dark brick walls. The cacophony of noises of the mass of boys messing about in the playground grew louder as I approached. As well as me there were several groups of boys on the pathway. They larked about roughly and noisily as they went. There were two fourth year prefects standing at the end of the pathway, one on each side. They were wearing the full school uniform. Blue blazer, grey trousers, silly hat etc. They both sported a shiny badge depicting their authority. One of them was a fairly decent kid. The other was a bit of a bully and he was armed with a twelve inch ruler with which he swatted the odd passing boy. The victim would be either a first or second year boy. I passed by the prefects and onto the tarmac playground without incident.

As I walked I surveyed the buildings and play ground area of the school. The main building was a two storied, square block of about sixteen classrooms. At the back of the block there was an annex building that was used as a sport hall, (used only by those kids that had sports kit.) There was another, smaller annex at the end and to the right of the main block. This was the dinning-come-assembly hall. That annex and the main block formed an L shape of buildings. Within the L shape, there was a small area of neglected garden that fringed one edge of the walled in playground. The main block was built of a combination of smooth red house bricks and dull, grey, monolithic blocks. The annex buildings looked temporary and didn't match the main block of the school. Along the front of the block on the ground floor was a wooden colonnade which gave access to the ground floor classrooms. The upper floor had a creaky, wooden balcony. The classrooms were all more or less identical. They were dismal. They were furnished with tatty old desks and chairs. The walls were bare bricked and had been lacquered to a high gloss. The windows were Georgian style and huge. Many of the glass pains were cracked. The teachers end consisted of a desk and chair, a free-standing easel and black board and a cupboard. All of the class-rooms stunk of schoolboys and disinfectant; I loathed the whole bloody place vehemently.

I held my breath and quickened my pace as I passed the reeking, crumbling toilet block. Groups of boys numbering from two, to ten or so were dotted about the playground. The din of about three hundred boys filled the air and bounced from wall to building and back again. Most of the first years were grouped in an area close to the assembly hall. This was where the prefects were usually gathered. The second year kids preferred to hang about at the entrance to the collonade. The third years, of which I was one, occupied various locations around the playground area. The fourth year youthes had the privilege of the narrow path between the main block and the assembly hall. This gave access to the sports hall annex. There, they were out of sight of the prefects and teachers staff room. So if they had any fags they could smoke their heads off with impunity. There was an unwritten rule about the path. It was considered to be out of bounds to prefects.

To be sure, despite the difference in age and background, every boy in that underfunded, vastly inadequate school, had one thing in common. We were all eleven plus failures. Some didn't care. Some felt dejected. Most felt rejected. However, in the fulness of time, all would realise that they had been severely shafted by an uncaring, biased and totally inadequate system of education.

I joined four of my classmates who were larking about in the middle of the playground. They were doing the usual pushing and shoving and trying to wrestle each other roughly to the ground. The skylarking was interspersed with a colourful mix of verbal obsenities. I threw a crude early morning greeting in their direction, but it fell upon deaf ears. I didn't join in with the wrestling. I stood watching but I wasn't seeing, my mind was elsewhere. I was still in a foul mood; I did notice however, when the noisy fooling about ceased abruptly.

My pals looked alarmed. They were looking past me, behind me; Suddenly, I was pushed violently from behind! I gasped with the shock of it. The wind was all but knocked out of me. My head snapped painfully back as I shot forward, almost careering into the group of friends. Somehow, I managed to keep my feet. The pain in my kneck and back was knifing, my heart was pounding. I stood for a moment or two breathing deeply; I was shaking from the sudden shock of the push. I tried to gather myself; I turned round slowly and cautiously. I knew instinctively who had pushed me. Sensibly, my friends faded back. I was on my own. The demand was made in low, menacing tones. 'Gimme a pen ya skinny little git!'

Chris Hanson was the boy that did the pushing. He was a fourth year. He was big, fat and pug ugly. He was notorious for being a particularly nasty bully. He was typical of all bullies, He would only pick on smaller and- or, weaker kids.

'I SAID GIMMIE A PEN YOU LITTLE BASTARD!' He yelled, his features twisted in forced rage. He drew closer; I was in a no-win situation. If I didn't give the slob my pen, pain would be inflicted by means of twisted arms and gut punching and Hanson wouldn't be satisfied untill I pleaded for mercy. If I did hand over the pen, the result would be the same. Pain and humiliation. I wasn't sure which was worse, the pain or the humiliation.

Although I was afraid and still shaky, I manged to control my voice. I stated evenly, 'I've only got one pen and I need it for myself.' Hanson was taken aback. He wasn't used to defiance from third year kids. He lunged at me, grabbed my lapels and dragged me upwards, almost lifting me off my feet. My face was within a couple of inches of his. His big face was mottled with puss filled spots and blackheads. His plump, moist top lip had a thin line of black wispy hair growing above it. His nose was wide and shiny. The stink of his breath turned my stomache. His tiny, pig-like eyes stared hard into mine. 'Gimme the pen,' he hissed through brown, rotting teeth. I stared back with contempt. For the first time in my life I experienced the emotion of real hatred.

After shaking me about until his arms began to ache, Hanson shoved me violently away. I staggered backwards and lost my footing. I half broke the fall with my hands.

All the same, the impact of the fall jarred my spine. The unyielding tarmac was cold, my wrists throbbed. I fought the pain by fighting back the tears; Hanson glared down at me, his face contorted in an evil grin. I glared back through moist eyes and with hatred in my heart. He had pushed once too often; He had pushed me too far.

After easing myself up into a sitting position, I massaged the small of my back. I then masaged my wrists. Whist massaging, I stared steadily at the cretinous oaf. He was laughing moronically. He was laughing in such a way that he couldn't fail to draw attention to his achievement. His laughing blinded him to the look of determined hatred in my eyes. Gradualy, the heat in my blood cooled and I calmed down. I got slowly to my feet. Hanson's laughter dwindled to an inane giggling. It stopped abruptly when he noticed that the fear in my eyes had been replaced with cold loathing.

"Come on ya little rat, hand over the pen!' His rasping voice sounded a little shaky, perhaps nervous. Slowly and purposely, I took out the pen from the inside pocket of my jacket. Slowly and purposefully, I proffered the pen. Hanson reached for it. Before his grubby hand got to it, I let it drop to the ground. Before the pen had stopped bouncing, I stamped on it. The cheap plastic split and splintered; Hanson was stunned! He looked from my face to the smashed pen several times befor fixing his incredulous gaze upon me. He then blustered stupidly, 'you did that on purpose ya scrawny little bastard!' 'No kidding,' I hissed through clamped teeth.

Although I was afraid, there was no way that I was going to back down. No matter what the cost, I wasn't going to take any more shoving around from Hanson and his like. Hanson daren't back down. He would have lost too much face because when I smashed the pen, a murmur rippled through the crowd of boys that, without us noticing, had gathered around Hanson and myself. The crowd was expectant; The punch came suddenly and seemingly from nowhere! I was caught off-guard. The speed of the fat slob supprised me. Instinctively, I rolled with the punch. It caught me a glancing blow above the right temple. Pain lanced through my skull. I was slightly dazed. I fought to gather my thoughts. Shaking my head, I back peddled.

As I back peddled, I thought of my Uncle Tom. I recalled some help and advice he had given me. It was after a fight I had been in. I had lost the fight and was badly knocked about. Uncle Tom took it upon himself to teach me how to look after myself in a scrap. He was a rough old diamond and a hard, punishing task-master. His earnest words came back to me. 'If you have to fight, fight hard and fast! Always punch straight! Aim high, never swing wildly and only back off so as to get wind!' I remembered looking up at his fearsome, battered features. His vast experience was evident.

My backward movement was halted by the crowd of eagerly waiting boys. Hanson stood glaring at me. Although he wasn't used to resistance from the likes of me, he seemed composed. After all, I was just a skinny little rat! He was clenching and unclenching his heavy hands confidently. As I weighed him up, more of my Uncle's wise words came to my mind. 'Keep balanced! Keep your fists high and clenched tight! Keep the rest of your body loose! Don't stand like a lemon, keep on the move at all times!'

I planted my left foot forward and leaned forward to balance my weight evenly. I clenched my fists tightly. The knuckles showed white. I began circling Hanson. I ignored his loud guffaw. I moved deftly on the balls of my feet, one step at a time, never crossing steps. Hanson looked from side to side as the crowd of boys closed ranks around us. They began chanting. 'OI, OI, OI.' More boys joined the throng on hearing the fight chant! I was amazed at how calm and focussed I felt. I clamped my teeth firmly together. My eyes never wavered from my target.

I lowered my fists for an instant. It was a feint! Hanson made his move! He lunged at me and swung his left fist in a wide arc! I ducked under the haymaker with ease! He was off balance! I stepped in and hit him with two wicked left jabs! I felt his spongy lips crush and the hardness of his teeth as my fist smashed into his loose mouth! I was only vaguely aware of the crowd as they roared with excitement! Blood poored from Hansons split lips. He was glancing rapidly from side to side. I could see tears in his eyes. I felt drunk with elation! I felt no pity for the wretched coward, no remorse for my actions. I moved in for another assault!

Hanson made a feeble attempt at a feint with his right hand. I saw what was coming. He lashed out with his right foot! I skipped back out of range of the heavy boot! He was off balance again and stumbling on to me. I hit him with two more stiff, arrow straight jabs! Both made solid contact beneath his right eye! I then threw a right cross that my Uncle Tom would have been proud of! The soft, pug nose flattened under the impact! Hanson was reeling. His eyes glistened with tears. Without mercy or compunction, I moved in to finish him.

I felt as if I was moving in slow motion. I had all the time in the world. Blinded by tears and blood, Hanson was defenceless against the furious barrage of well aimed, solid punches that I pounded him with! I stopped the pummelling when his legs buckled and he dropped to his knees. An emulsion of blood, tears and snot dripped from his swelling features. He gasped two chocking words. 'No more!' I stared down at the pathetic bully. I stared at the result of my controlled, cold blooded fury. I had not the slightest feeling of pity. On the contrary, I felt strangely satisfied. Fulfilled even.

The raucus din of the mob had receded to a mumbling whisper. Hanson was lying on his side groaning. I lowered my bloodied fists. They smarted when I unclenched them. I hung my aching arms at my sides. My breathing seemed loud. The sweat dried on me. I began shaking; 'Watch it!' Whispered somebody hoarsely. The mob dispersed in seconds. 'YOU LAD, STAND WHERE YOU ARE!'

The large, lumbering frame of Mr Devril the woodwork teacher approached. His face looked like thunder. As he neared, the bell for assembly sounded. I looked up at the towering teacher. He looked from me to the bleeding, sobbing Hanson and back again. He had a look of disgust on his big, florid face. He thrust his hands hard into the pockets of his tweed jacket and said in low manacing tones. 'Wipe that evil grin off of your face and report to the Headmasters office after assembly boy!' As I walked away I heard him say to Hanson. 'You picked a wrong'un this time didn't you lad.'

I examined my hands. They hurt a little but they weren't to badly damaged. I almost bumped into one of my friends. It was Dicky Lewin. He was known as Windy

Lewin. He was a pleasant kid. He was always smartly dressed and wore loud ties. His hair was flattened to his head by about a half pound of grease. His face was round and shiny and it had a permanent smile on it. He was blessed with a remarkable and enviable gift. He was able to break wind at will! Hence the nick name, Windy. I smiled at him, he didn't smile back. His face was pale and he was shaking. Slowly, he reached out his left hand and took my right hand. He then turned my hand palm up and placed the smashed pen onto it and closed my fingers over the pieces. Then he turned about and walked away; From that day on, Dick Lewin never spoke to me again.

So there I was in the gloomy waiting room that led on to the Headmasters office awaiting punishment. The pungent odour of pipe tobacco and floor polish hung in the air. I felt nervous but elated. I thought about the amount of strokes of the cane I would recieve. Fighting at school was a definate no, no. Oddly enough though, bullying seemed to be acceptable. As it happened, caning did nothing to deter me from committing further offences of a similar nature. Little did I know that from that day on, fighting would become a major part of my life.

END

Deadly Error

If there is one situation that seafarers fear more than any other whilst at sea it is falling overboard. If the unfortunate seaman should survive the first few minutes of the ordeal, he has to endure the torture of watching as his ship, his home and all his shipmates disappearing over the distant horizon.

One can only imagine the rollercoaster of emotions that a situation like that could incur; Panic, fear, horror, loneliness and worst of all, the dreadful feeling of being abandoned.

This story is an attempt to portray, by means of my imagination and some experience, such a horrific situation. If I have come anywhere near to succeeding, I will be satisfied. I'll be happy to leave you, the reader to be the judge.

D Grieve

"Worse things happen at sea."

This is a saying that is often quoted at times of misfortune or mishap. The following narrative concerns one of the most terrifying ordeals that a mariner could possibly experience.

Part One
A short story by David Grieve

Our ship was cruising at optimum economical speed on a southerly course. Our approximate position was midway between the island of Madagascar to the east and Mozambique to the west on the eastern seaboard of the vast continent of Africa. We were roughly halfway through the Mozambique Channel. The sea was flat calm and the air was motionless.

The Persian Gulf, now known as the Gulf of Iran, was far behind us, as was the Red Sea, The Arabian Sea, the Gulf of Aden and many other exotic and not so exotic places in the middle and far east. We were on the next to penultimate leg of our long journey back to good old Blighty. On returning to Portsmouth, it would be a total of fifteen and a half months since I, and indeed the rest of the crew of the Tern, last sighted the beautiful and much missed coastline of southern England.

HMS Tern was a general purpose Frigate of two and a half thousand tons. Her crew consisted of about two hundred and eighty men including officers. She was a fine looking vessel and was capable of cutting the ocean at a fair lick and was spiked with lethal armament. The Captain was proud of his ship and was once heard to describe her as a 'feisty lass' and his crew as 'salty'. The crew were a happy, contented lot and I was proud to be counted as one of them.

On a particular night in 1966, I was standing on the quarterdeck leaning back on the after bulkhead. The time was 0010 hours, ten minutes into the middle watch. Above me, the overtaking light was burning brightly, lighting the after wash deck and casting shadows from the fittings and equipment thereon. The green painted deck was glistening wet and reflected the numerous abstract shapes of the deck fittings as they dripped the moisture of the humid tropical night. I had just begun my first stint as lifebuoy lookout for the watch. Lifebuoy lookout was a lonely duty and was known to any seaman in the Royal Navy that ever stood a watch on deck as, 'lifebuoy ghost'.

The lifebuoy ghost is stationed on the after end of the ship on the quarterdeck or, depending on the type of ship, the wash deck. His duties are fairly basic and mostly boring. However, his job is of the utmost importance. To describe it simply, the lifebuoy ghost is the last hope for any unfortunate soul that happens to fall overboard unobserved. Especially late at night when the upper deck is all but deserted; The ghosts' equipment consists of a loud hailer, a powerful flashlight and several means of communication to various departments of the ship, most importantly, a direct emergency line to the bridge and the officer of the watch. There are plenty of lifebuoys and floats at hand with salt water activated lights attached via lanyards. During working hours, the duties of the ghost falls to a member of the quarterdeck part of ship, that being his place of work.

The cool dampness of the after bulkhead soaked through the tough fabric of my work shirt and trousers, number eights as they were known. The heavy humidity annoyed and itched my face as it trickled off my hair, eyebrows and lashes. I checked the time again. It would be another 45 minutes before a bleary eyed rating would appear on deck to relieve me.

I leaned off of the bulkhead and began pacing to and fro athwart ships. As I paced, I pondered. I knew that there would be a break in the usual boredom of the watch as there was to be an exercise during the watch as specified in 'daily orders'. Daily orders were a print out of every thing that was to occur during the 24 hours following their issue. Like all orders in the service they had to be obeyed and or, adhered to without question. The exercise would take place at an unspecified time during the middle watch. It was to be a 'tactical evasion' exercise and consisted of the ship increasing speed at a rapid rate and being steered in a zigzag pattern in order to confuse an enemy and frustrate an attack from the air or from beneath us. The alterations in coarse would be inconsistent and severe. I mumbled to myself 'bring it on, lets have a change of routine'.

The mirror like sea was gloriously purple in the silver-blue light of an almost full moon and the inky blue of the night sky. Countless stars of varying brilliance and hue spangled the heavens like a twinkling rash. Shooting stars slashed the self-repairing fabric of the mysterious infinity that was the tropical canopy above me. The distant, almost indistinct horizon drew a line beneath the impossible to copy, celestial beauty.

I ceased my pacing, had a good stretch and vigorously brushed the moisture from my hair with my hands. The only sounds that could be heard were those of the sea reluctantly giving way to the powerful thrust of the ship and the low rhythmic throb of the ships twin engines, the shuddering power of which could be felt as the steel plates of the deck vibrated underfoot. I looked down the sixty foot length of the quarter deck and beyond the after guardrail. The ships wake stretched and narrowed brightly astern. It was arrow straight and was festooned with translucent jewels of green and turquoise phosphorus; It occurred to me that before long, the peace would be shattered and the helmsman would have his work cut out. I told myself to be aware and keep my wits about me.

I went over to the port guardrail. As I stepped out of the lee of the after bulkhead I felt the force of the fourteen-knot wind that was created by the ships' momentum. The wind was warm and carried the pungent odour of burnt fuel. I looked forward along the length of the port waist and then up at the super structure amidships. The port navigation light was burning brightly, as was the masthead steaming light, both easily seen from the horizon. I then decided to take a walk around the quarterdeck and do some routine checks.

To the uninitiated, walking around the upper deck of a ship of war could prove to be hazardous, even in daylight; Experienced seamen are used to the many obstacles and objects that protrude from the decks. There are also many pieces of equipment either permanently fixed or lashed in various locations on deck. Even old hands stub their toes and bark their shins from time to time. I stepped carefully as I made my way aft via the port side of the quarterdeck.

As I moved aft, the sound of the ships propellers began to get the better of the rumbling of the engines. The momentum-induced breeze cooled me a little. I perused the deck as I walked. I paid special attention to the guardrails, checking the tension of the topmost steel cable. The guardrails were often being removed or adjusted for various tasks as required during the ships commission. As a result, the cable can become stretched or frayed and the bottle screw adjusters can ware. It was strictly forbidden for anybody to lean on the guardrails at any time. Leaning on the stanchions was a safer option.

As I neared the stern guardrail, the noise of the propellers grew to a steady roar. On reaching the rail I positioned myself behind a stanchion and looked down over the transom; Below, a dramatic, battle was taking place between man made mechanical might and the immense power of nature. The placid sea was thrashed into a roaring, jade coloured tempest by the rapidly turning screws. Large flecks of fluorescence danced in the maelstrom. Before becoming mesmerised I lifted my Gaze. In the far distance, forks of lightning streaked to earth, momentarily splitting the heavens and blotting the stars. My eyes were fooled by the intensity of the blue-silver flashes, for they appeared to linger and spread wider.

I remained at the stem looking out to sea for five minutes or so before tearing myself away from the spectacular light show and making my way back to the lifebuoy station. I went via the starboard side, as I went I carried out more checks. All was well. Once back in the lee of the bulkhead I resumed pacing too and fro. White patches of salt crystals were already forming in the dents and nooks and crannies of the recently painted deck. It wouldn't be long before the deck and all its' fixtures and fittings would need another coat of paint. As I paced, I immersed myself in deep thought. As always, I went through the procedure to be followed in the unlikely event of a Man falling overboard. Those thoughts and many others besides helped to pass the somewhat boring time away.

My observations were interrupted when the rhythmic throbbing of the engines grew in volume. The water that was lying on the deck shivered as the vibration of the plates grew in intensity. The ship gained speed rapidly. The exercise had begun! It wouldn't be long before the ship began to yaw and heel at an alarming rate. I felt a pang of excitement as I anticipated the break in the monotony of steady cruising. I looked at my watch. It was 0053 hours. The first hour of my watch was almost up, as was my first stint of lifebuoy ghost. Two minutes later, my relief was on the quarterdeck.

He arrived via the port waist clutching a mug of tea in his meaty left hand. His name was Owen Morris. As his name indicated, he was a Welshman. He was born and bred in a coal mining district of the valleys and was very proud of it. He was big, boisterous and a keen rugby man. He had on a lightweight blue shirt that was open to his waist and a pair of cut down number eight trousers. On his feet was a pair of tatty leather sandals. A mop of unruly, black curly hair topped his large head. Depicted on his hairy, barrel-like chest was a tattoo of the Welsh national flag, beneath which, in large gothic letters, was the word 'CMRU'. As I looked at 'Taffy' I considered that it was a good thing that the dress code on board ship was very relaxed while at sea.

'Now then bucko, everything ok is it? He said in fine melodic tones.

'Yes everything's fine, everything's lashed and stowed at this end Taffy, nothing to report.' Owen yawned and stretched and said.

'Well then bucko, get yourself below, there's some fresh tea just been mashed.'

'Great, I'll see you in an hour then Taffy and don't forget, the ship will be riving all over the place shortly, so take care'. I emphasised the 'take care'.

The smiling Welshman gave me the thumbs up, so I made my way forward by way of the starboard waist.

To get below, I headed for a watertight door that led on to a hatch that led directly down to the galley and dinning flat. The door was situated on the bulkhead halfway down the starboard waist. Due to the increase in speed, the wind was now much stronger. As I walked, I held firmly onto the grab rail that ran the length of the bulkhead. I leaned into the wind and reminded myself again that the ship could veer and heel to port or starboard at any time. The wind felt pleasant as it rushed by, drying off the moisture in my hair and on my face. My body was cooling pleasantly. I was passing a door to one of the many deck stores when I reached out with my right hand and took hold of the starboard guardrail. It was unusually slack! Dangerously slack! I stopped and surveyed the offending section of cable. The bottle screw was loose! It was only holding by the last few threads of the ringbolt attached to the stanchion.

In view of the fact that I had already warned myself twice and reminded Taffy of the danger, what I did next was unutterably, inexcusably stupid; I should have waited for the ship to make its first course alteration before attempting to take the slack out of the guardrail. After warning myself twice, and my reminder to Owen, I acted like a green fool. I don't know what possessed me. Equally moronic was the fact that I had failed to notice that the door to the deck store behind me wasn't properly clipped shut! I began working on the bottle screw. I worked quickly. I wasn't quick enough!

The ship veered suddenly to port and heeled acutely to starboard. The whole vessel shuddered as the keel was forced out of shape by the tremendous forces that were placed upon it by engines, rudder angle and ocean. Instinctively, I leaned into the angle and made to retain my grip on the grab rail. The heavy steel door struck me heavily between the shoulder blades. The pain shot up and down my spine but was quickly forgotten as I pitched headlong over the side! I didn't have far to fall before I hit the water due to the angle of the ships side.

The instant I went under, I was dragged downwards. I thought I was going to die there and then! I felt certain I was going to drown, The certainty of death by drowning was quickly replaced with the more dreadful certainty Of being smashed into small pieces by the huge, thrashing blades of the ships propellers; I had heard it said, that when a person is close to death, the events of their entire life flash through their mind. This was not the case for me. My mind was totally absorbed by the horror of an agonising, gory death.

I thought at the time that it would have been better if I had been rendered unconscious by the blow from the door. In the event, I was aware of everything that was happening to me; I was being buffeted and spun like a top in a roaring, green-white cloud of turbulence as the air above the surface was being dragged into the violent battle between metal and water. The racket was horrifying. I thought my eardrums would burst. Worse still, I was dreadfully aware that the stem of the ship was swinging rapidly to starboard and that I was in its path! I was totally powerless to do anything against the awesome forces.

I closed my eyes as the tremendous cacophony of engines, propellers and furious sea grew to a thundering crescendo. My helpless body spun, pitched and rolled faster and faster. My lungs ached for air. If I could have screamed, I would have screamed. If I could have cried, I would have cried. I prayed for unconsciousness. I begged for a quick death.

As it happened, I was neither drowned nor chopped to pieces. To this day I am unsure why or what happened that caused me to be spared from what I thought would be certain death. However, I somehow survived the initial, fearful ordeal of falling overboard. Since those fateful moments I have had several theories as to how I got away with my life. My initial thoughts were of some kind of miracle. Fate was another, as was pure luck. In the end, Logic told me that I owed my survival to physics alone. The swift, mighty swing of the ships stern must have created a powerful underwater pressure wave that pushed my body far enough away from the screws so that the ship passed by leaving me free and clear of the stern.

Since hitting the water, I can't have been under for much more than a horrifying, chaotic two minutes or so. It seemed a whole lot longer. The next thing I remember was seeing a bright, silver light shimmering above me.

Popping up like a cork I broke surface and gulped lungs full of welcome tropical air. I also gulped a goodly amount of seawater. I retched, spluttered and puked until the foul tasting liquid was clear of my stomached and mouth. Once I composed myself, I fixed my streaming eyes on the friendly bright moon in the placid starlit sky. My head was still whirling. I tried to gather my thoughts. Suddenly, I was dragged under again by a fierce undertow! It pulled me along in the wake of the ship. I tried to swim against it, but my efforts were puny against the strength of the undertow. I had no choice but to let myself be dragged along. I started to feel panicky, I needn't have. Shortly, the strength of the undertow began to diminish. I caught sight of the moonlight and swam towards it. I was deceptively deep, it took longer to reach the surface than I expected. I swam hard. Once I got there, I didn't gulp in the air. I did my best to breath normally and not swallow seawater again.

I struggled to stay afloat in the turbulence of the ships wake. There was a hissing sound all about me as millions of tiny bubbles burst upon the surface. I was still alive and for a brief moment I was filled with euphoria. I gathered my thoughts; Soon, the extreme seriousness of my predicament dawned upon me. With my line of sight being close to the surface of the sea, my horizon was but a short distance from me. Although I could hear the rumble of engines, I couldn't see the ship. I turned in the water as quickly as I could. I turned my head rapidly from side to side in an effort to catch sight of my ship. I was beginning to panic; I caught sight of her masthead steaming light. She seemed a long way distant! She had altered course and increased speed. The Tern was capable of over 35 knots. She would soon disappear from my sight!

Total panic took hold and drove me into a frenzy of foolish action. I began yelling at the top of my voice, 'STOP! STOP! STOP THE FUCKING SHIP'! I repeated over and over. The shouting graduated to screaming. I flailed my arms about like a madman and beat the surface of the water with my hands and arms in a frantic, futile attempt to catch the attention of my shipmate, Owen Morris, the lifebuoy ghost.

I have no idea how long I kept up the pointless, energy sapping madness. I do know that I had left myself almost drained of energy and that my throat and mouth were dry and sore; When the masthead steaming light disappeared from my sight, a feeling of utter desperation swept over me. I began yelling again. 'DON'T LEAVE ME HERE! PLEASE DON'T LEAVE ME HERE! FOR PITYS SAKE HELP ME! HELP ME!' I raised my arms to wave them. I sank like a shackle and I swallowed what felt like a pint of seawater. The natural buoyancy of the Indian Ocean didn't slow my descent. Having wasted my breath and my energy panicking, it didn't take long for my lungs to start hurting and my head to throb more painfully. My arms and legs felt like lead. Before very long, my lungs felt as though they were about to burst and my head explode. I was drowning!

Significant memories of my 25 years of life flitted in and out of my mind in rapid succession. The good times and the bad times of my past appeared in my minds eye for an instant and then were gone. Images of my parents, my Brother and my Sisters came and went. My Mother with her beaming smile, then weeping bitterly. My Father, grim as ever. My younger brother and me at the rivers edge, muddy and laughing. My older sister, lounging as usual. My younger sister, quiet, lonely. Visions of my school and the teachers, good and bad, mostly bad. My old friends, my motorbike. My old enemies, the fights, running from the police, joining the Navy. All those visions were interspersed with many others. I felt the happiness and the sadness of my past in my heart. I felt the thrills and spills of my short life. I felt the awful pain.

Pain, I felt pain. The pain was intense and growing in intensity, approaching agony. My skull felt as if it were in a slowly tightening vice. My ribs were tightening and closing around the organs within their cage. My stomach felt full to bursting point. I was sinking deeper into the depths of the Mozambique Channel. I was close to unconsciousness.

It must have been some kind of primordial instinct that still exists in the human subconscious and the now, excruciating pain that snapped me out of my stupor. My brain, being starved of oxygen wasn't functioning properly. Instinct took over! Pain and fear driven adrenalin coursed through my veins. My will to live was strong and drove me into action. I began swimming. I had not a clue as to which direction the surface was, I just assumed that it was above my head so, that was the direction I swam. To say I swam is a misnomer. I kicked with my legs and flapped my arms like a demented penguin. I moved my throbbing head from side to side and up and down in the desperate hope of glimpsing, through blurred, aching eyes, the faintest glimmer of light. If I saw light below me I new that all would be lost, I had no choice but to continue in the direction I was going.

My strength began to ebb as the flow of adrenalin began depleting. The pain-wracked effort of my struggle became almost unbearable. My efforts to swim became pathetic. I felt as though I had been submerged for ages. My body was a ton weight. My eyelids felt like lead curtains. With a mighty effort I raised my head and looked upwards.

The light seemed to burst through my pupils and illuminate my entire brain! At first I thought I was hallucinating. Then my feeble thoughts turned to the fabled light that led to some kind of heavenly paradise. The friendly, most welcome light was no hallucination, nor was it the way to an afterlife. The source of the light was the beautiful, the wonderful moon. The surface of the sea was no more than two feet above me! One more agonising 'penguin flap' and my head broke the surface!

On feeling the air on my face, I filled my lungs to capacity with the desperately needed gasses of life. The effect of the oxygen rush to my brain was phenomenal. It was as if it had been injected with pure alcohol. At first it felt wonderful, exhilarating, elevating. Then, after a short while, calming. The awful pressure in my head and chest cavity eased. The effect of oxygen replenishing my blood and the knowledge that against all the odds I was still alive filled me with elation. My heart rate steadied and the pain in my limbs became tolerable. I breathed deeply, hungrily. I blew salt water and mucus out of my mouth and sore nostrils. My eyes became less blurred and gradually clearer.

The initial rush of oxygen to my brain levelled off. My head continued to throb. It felt as though I was suffering the result of a good 'run ashore'. I had a bad hangover.

If only! Fortunately, I was a strong swimmer. I was treading water. It was an automatic action. Eventually, my head cleared completely, I began thinking; I knew that I was in dire straights. I also realised that if I got into another state of panic, the odds of my survival would be radically shortened. There was no way of removing the gut wrenching fear within me. At all costs, I had to overcome that fear, and try, no matter how difficult, to stay calm and to think clearly.

I scanned my limited horizon. I strained my eyes for a sighting of the speeding ship. I knew in my heart that there was little chance of seeing her. However, I listened intently across the flat, silent surface of the moonlit sea. After a few moments, I picked up the faint, distant rumble of her engines. I ducked my head under water. Over the pounding in my ears I could hear the Hydrophone effect of her screws as they battled against the sea; Of course, by this time all feelings of elation had left me. I had to mentally fight hard against the feeling of panic that tried to take charge. I fought it off. I breathed deeply, all the way down into my gut. Fear remained and I was well aware that it would be ever present whilst I was in such a deadly situation. I would have to deal with it.

My next thoughts were of the negative type. I thought how unutterably stupid I was for getting myself into my perilous situation. Why oh why did I try to fix that fucking guardrail at such a dangerously unpredictable time? Why didn't I wait? What was the hurry? What on earth possessed me to act in such a foolish manner? I was an experienced seaman for fuck sake! The thoughts were getting loud in my head. I was loosing my temper and getting agitated. 'SHUT UP! SHUT UP YOU BLOODY

FOOL'! I shouted those words and shook my head to rid my mind of the pointless ranting. Then, as I recall, I did a very odd thing. I looked all around me so as to see if anybody had heard my outburst! There I was, somewhere in the middle of the Mozambique channel, part of the vast Indian Ocean, worrying in case somebody had heard me shouting! Could there be anything more ludicrous than to consider that I could be heard in the loneliest of lonely situations. I began chuckling. The chuckling graduated to hearty laughter. Soon, I was laughing until the tears ran down my cheeks. Gradually, the tears of mirth gave way to sobbing tears of dark sorrow as the powerful emotion of self-pity engulfed me.

I don't know how much time I wasted feeling sorry for myself, but somehow I managed to get my thoughts away from my pathos and on to a course of more positive thinking. I told myself to pull myself together, to stop acting like a stupid schoolboy. I drew in a great, shuddering breath. Then, speaking aloud and with severity, I gave myself an order. 'Now then man, think positively!' Act positively!' I repeated the order over and over until the negative thoughts were all but cleared from my mind.

I had to make myself understand my plight. This was easy. I was in deep shit as well as water! However, there was a chance of rescue. I had to believe that fact! The odds were long, but there was a chance. I had to try and shorten those odds. My next thoughts were of my physical condition; I had a throbbing headache and some pain in my ribcage. My joints ached. My muscles had been strained but not pulled. The same went for my tendons. Although I couldn't see it, I must have had an almighty bruise on my back. The pain was tolerable. My sight was slightly blurred but I reckoned my eyes would clear shortly. My hearing was fine. Considering what I had just been through, I was in pretty good shape.

Next, I considered my clothing. My number eight shirt was completely bereft of buttons. My trousers were mainly intact. The belt loops were ripped and the lanyard that was threaded through them was lost, as was my jack knife, which was attached to the lanyard. My deck boots and my socks were gone also.

I trod water steadily as I pondered on the more complicated aspects of the situation. First I had to try to figure out the length of time I had been in the water. How far distant was the ship? Most importantly, how long would it be before it was discovered that I was missing? I looked at my watch. Fortunately, it had a good quality strap. Unfortunately though, the business part of the bloody thing was useless. The so called water proof, shock proof, tested to such and such a depth piece of crap was water logged. Perhaps I expected too much from the 45 dollar, bought in Hong Kong, lump of junk. 45 bucks HK was the equivalent of about ten quid sterling. Serves me right!

Although I felt as if I had been in the sea for ages, in reality, it couldn't have been longer than about 10 minutes, 15 at most. I was thankful that the weather was in my favour. I hoped upon hope that it remained so. The moon and stars were still bright, the sea flat calm. Visibility was good and there was not the hint of a breeze. I turned myself in the water so that the moon was off to my right. I made the move so that I was facing roughly in the direction the Tern was heading. I assumed that she had remained on a mean course during the exercise. I recalled that the moon was off to my left when I was on the quarterdeck, it wouldn't have moved much in the last 15 minutes or so. I glanced behind me. Lightning was still splitting the dark sky to the northeast. That was one of the few times that I never took time to marvel at the beauty of the tropical night sky.

Knowing that the ship was heading in a southerly direction, south, southwest to be accurate, I was satisfied that I was facing south. I began to rethink my chances of survival. The thoughts filled me with dread but I had to think above those feelings. I repeated my stem order several times in my mind. By now, it was painfully obvious that Taffy had neither seen nor heard me fall over the side. That was not at all surprising considering the racket the ship was making as it increased speed and heeled hard over.

Besides that, the last thing on Taffy's mind would be that anybody, especially an experienced hand like me should fall off the ship! Who would? He would have been preoccupied with trying to remain on his feet and keeping the tea in his mug.

No other member of the watch on deck would miss me until Taffy gave the alarm. The two assigned lifebuoy ghosts took their rest hour in the dinning flat. The rest of the watch stayed up on the boat deck amidships. Taffy would expect me to relieve him at 0055 hours. At my failure to turn to, he would give me a few minutes grace before informing the officer of the watch of my absence. It would be around 45 minutes time from my act of crass stupidity before anybody onboard the Tern would know something was amiss. By that time, I would have been in the brine for approximately one hour.

I continued my steady, rhythmic leg and arm action treading water. As I did so, I made some more rough calculations. Still assuming that the ship was steaming at 25 knots plus and that. she was keeping on her mean coarse, 190 degrees, or there about and, that I reckoned that by now, I had been in the water for around thirty minutes, give or take a few, I figured that the Tern would be at most, 15 miles distant from my position, perhaps only 12; All my positive thinking was paying off. I felt much easier about my predicament. My confidence in being rescued had grown twofold. The odds were shortening. In the all but total silence of the humid night I visualised what would happen when the 'man overboard' alarm was raised.

There is a specific routine to be followed in the rare event of some fool falling off the ship. If not already on the bridge, the Captain would be roused from his cabin. At the same time the bosun's mate would be sent below to roust out another watch of seamen. The helmsman would be ordered to bring the ship about and reverse course. The telegraphs would be rung to 'full ahead' and maximum revolutions would be wound on. In the meantime, a search party would be mustered and the ship searched from stem to stern. The search party would consist of two hands from each branch or department of the ship. The middle watchmen would be questioned as to who the last person to have seen me and at what time.

Once it was established that I was definitely not on board, a priority signal would be transmitted to any and all vessels within range requesting assistance in a patterned search. Extra radar plotters would be turned too; The chances of detecting me on radar were miniscule. My head would be no more significant on a radar screen than the thousands of other dots thereon. The human head is not a very good reflector of radar waves. However, I could be confident that the operators would give it their best. The most experienced sonar control operatives would man the sonar control room. They would be deployed on a listening only search. The human body is not a good reflector of sonar transmissions. The men in the control room were messmates of mine. 'Anti submarine warfare' was my specialist qualification. It went without saying that those men would also do their utmost to detect me. Every available pair of binoculars would be issued to all the spare hands on deck Powerful searchlights would be deployed. 'An emergency boats crew' would muster and stand by. Cooks would be ordered to the galley in order to supply tea, coffee and sandwiches. The ship would become a hive of determined activity in the space of a few minutes. There would be many volunteers from the other watches. They would be ordered below to get their sleep. The search could go on for a long time. Wakeful, clear minds and eyes maybe required. My mind boggled at the thought of all this frantic, but well executed activity brought about by a silly bastard who failed to use his common sense! Guilt stabbed at my heart.

It would quickly be established that the loose guard-rail and the swinging bulkhead door was the place that I went over the side. An estimate of the time I fell would be fixed. That information would be passed up to the Skipper and most importantly, the Navigating Officer. He would be on the bridge in his tiny chart room poring over his chart of the Mozambique Channel. To me, at that time, he was my best hope of survival. He would put all of his skill and experience, by means of methods that are, and have always been a mystery to me, to indicate an area of ocean that I would most likely be adrift in. His calculations would be given to the Skipper. As the ship neared the established area, speed would be reduced and the search would be officially initiated.

My life depended on the vigilance of my shipmates and the skill and judgement of the Captain and his lieutenants. I had been a member of the ships' company of H.M.S. Tern for well over two years. I knew the crew well. It was comforting to know that I could rely on every man jack of them to do their utmost to locate and rescue me. As well as myself, I owed it to all of those stalwart men to do every thing in my power to survive. If I didn't, it would not be for the lack of trying. All those musings gave me much food for thought.

I made a conscious check of the rate that I was treading water. I slowed it down a little; I considered that trying to keep track of time with any degree of accuracy was a waste of time. There was also nothing to be gained on trying to keep myself facing in the direction the ship had gone. I needed to put my conscious and physical efforts into staying afloat. I was at the mercy of the currents and the tidal flow of the channel. Also, the weather could change for the worse. Swimming was not an option. I needed to conserve my energy. Anyhow, where and in what direction could I swim? No, I told myself, just keep treading water.

I reassessed my situation. I felt optimistic. It was a good thing that I had always kept myself fit. I enjoyed most kinds of sports and given the opportunity would take part in most team games. I was well muscled, supple and had developed a good degree of stamina due to such activities as cross-country and distance running; Keeping the level of consumption of tobacco and booze to a sensible level over the years was another point in my favour. The temptation to smoke and drink too much could become an occupational hazard for personnel serving in the R.N. At that point in time however, I would have given anything for a tot of rum and a roll of strong tickler. My thoughts boosted my belief that I would be rescued. I sighed deeply. I considered that the odds had swung a tad more in my favour.

Part Two

The warm salt water went a long way toward reducing the tension and aches and pains in my muscles and tendons. Nothing however, could reduce the fear within me! It was part of the situation. It was up to me to keep the stomach churning pangs in check. I did this by keeping my mind occupied and concentrating on nothing more than what was immediately important. I dared not think too far ahead. I breathed deeply and steadily and I trod water at the optimum rate as was necessary to keep me afloat. I slowly turned in the water through 360 degrees. I scanned my horizon for any sign of navigation lights. Although hopeful, I wasn't too disappointed at seeing nothing. I looked skyward; the moon was lowering and waning. The stars twinkled and winked at me. The electrical storm that had violently streaked and ripped the night sky to the north had eased its' vehemence and was now lighting its' stage with sheet lightning. Apart from the sound of the distant, ghostly rumble of thunder as it rolled slowly over the ocean, and the occasional soft, rippling sounds of my movements, silence reigned; I had never before experienced such a depth of silence, lonely, ghostly, oppressive silence.

I carried out another full circle scan. Still nothing. My disappointment was short lived. Something else grabbed my attention. Although I tried to ignore it, I felt the weight of fatigue creeping into my arms and legs. It was time to remove my trousers. I cast my mind back to my basic training. Naturally, part of that training was about survival in the event of ending up adrift in the open sea without a life preserver. With training, it is possible to use ones clothing as an aid to buoyancy. Naturally, being able to use the technique would depend upon weather conditions and sea state. I was fortunate, weather and sea state were in my favour.

I had difficulty unfastening the cloth cross-straps of my trousers due to the fact that they were soaking wet and it wasn't easy to work on them whilst trying to stay afloat at the same time. With patience, I managed to get straps and buttons undone and remove my duds. The next task was to refasten the buttons and cross straps. Then, I tied the end of each trouser leg in as tight a knot as I could manage. I then re-buttoned the fly and knotted the straps, leaving the waistband open. The knot tying left my hands a bit sore. My flesh was already beginning to soften in the salt water. All the same it was worth it. My efforts gained me a serviceable life preserver. All I had to do then was fill it with air. I achieved this by crossing my arms and gripping the duds by the waistband at the seams. I then had to turn so as to place the trousers, with the legs outstretched, behind my head. Then, with one quick, smooth movement I hauled the trousers up high, over my head and down into the water in front of me. Air was dragged into the knotted legs and then I screwed up the waistband to form a seal there. The successful procedure left me with a pair of heavy cotton balloons that could remain inflated for up to twenty minutes or so. Although the devise worked well, there was one major drawback. The effort required to refill the float repeatedly would be energy sapping.

I manoeuvred the balloons under my armpits. I eased my weight onto them and eased off treading water. I floated. I breathed a deep, loud sigh. The relief for my aching limbs felt wonderful, exquisite. After luxuriating for a few moments, I suddenly felt twice as vulnerable as before I had removed my trousers. It must have been psychological. My head was suddenly filled with a barrage of horrifying, demoralising thoughts! Fearful images of sleek, powerful, razor toothed sharks engaged in a ferocious, gory, feeding frenzy swam through my head. Thousands of shimmering Jellyfish streaming long, scorching tentacles drifted around my legs. Intricately patterned, tenacious, lethal sea snakes stealthily approached. My minds eye watched as a wretched, lifeless body sank into to the unforgiving, black depths.

I shook my head and willed my mind to push the horrendous thoughts out. I became aware that my rate of breathing had become shorter and faster. Also, I had started treading water again, erratically. I steadied the rate immediately but continued to tread water. I closed my eyes tightly and tried to force my thoughts into a different, pleasant pattern. I thought of my home. I cast my mind back to my childhood, to when my home was a wonderful place to be. I visualised a cold, rainy evening on the street that I lived. Brightly lit shops cast their light across the shiny pavement. Huge, red, trolley busses trundled by, their smeared, steamed up windows lit yellow. Blue sparks flew from the conductor poles and the overhead power cables. The happy sounds of song and laughter emitting from the Red Lion pub on the corner. I smiled as I recalled the muddy, chaotic, twenty-a-side football matches that I played in at the local park, and the one and only goal I ever scored. Equally chaotic games of cricket were played in the heat of glorious English summers, using makeshift kit and with far too many players on the pitch. I remembered the feeling of great achievement I got when I scored a total of three runs off eighteen balls. I thought fondly of the good days of family life, when we were close. The long, riverside walks on warm evenings. Chewing on cockles and mussels, crunching salty crisps. Drinking fizzy lemonade, the games, the fun and the joyful laughter.

My fond reminiscences were interrupted when I felt an awful feeling of nausea turn my stomach. My heart skipped a beat as my body rose. The ever-present fear lurking within me leapt to the fore. Moments later, I realised I was being lifted by a long, rolling tiderip. The fear abated a little. The gentle wave carried me up its' eight foot slope to its' crest and then eased me down the other side, by which time, the effects of 'mal de mare' had left me. I chuckled nervously as I bobbed up and down in the aftermath of the friendly roller. For some reason that was beyond my comprehension, an odd feeling of sadness swept over me as I watched the glistening wave roll away into the darkness. I wondered if it would grow into a massive, destructive tidal wave that would break and crash onto some distant coastline. Or would it dwindle to harmless ripples that children could noisily frolic and splash around in.

The sea gradually settled to mirror flat again. I checked my float for air content. It would need refilling shortly.

I carried out another scan. I sighed deeply, there was nothing in sight. I spent at least a minute listening intently for the slightest sound of screw or engine. Absolute silence reigned. Doubt of my rescue began nibbling at my heart. I said allowed. 'Don't be daft, you'll be out of this soon; my words didn't sound very convincing.

My stomach rumbled. It sounded inordinately loud in the lonely silence. It had been several hours since I had last eaten. Lack of food was the least of my problems at that time. Lack of water was a far more worrying prospect. A healthy young man could go at least two weeks without food and· remain in fair condition, if he took it easy that is. Without water however, no matter how fit he may be, a man could not expect to live for more than a few days. I began to get depressed. I had to raise my spirits. I told myself that there was no way that I would be adrift long enough to die of thirst and that soon, I would hear the sound of my sea going home as it approached to pick me up. I formed a mental picture of the occasion. Everybody was pointing and laughing at me.

I went through the procedure to re-inflate my float. The effort left me a little breathless. My neck and my limbs were aching sorely. Physical strain, fear and tension were beginning to ware at me. I took several deep breaths and tried to relax as much as I could; I wondered what the time was, how long had I been in the water? It seemed an awful long time. I would soon have a rough idea of the time because at around about 0300 hours, the sun would start brightening the sky to the east. I scanned round again; there was no sign of light other than the odd sheet of lightning that persisted to the north. I looked up at the waning moon. I smiled at it and asked, 'what are my odds now my friend?' The silence was more oppressive. I closed my eyes to rest them. They were beginning to fill with tears. I almost dozed off.

Suddenly, I felt an odd sensation in my legs! It felt as though an under current was flowing around and through my legs, I could feel the pressure. It wasn't very strong, but pressure it most definitely was! The almost dormant fear leapt from within my heart and gripped my every fibre! I glanced anxiously about me! I had no idea what I was looking for! I didn't want to find anything! I told myself that it was just another tiderip! Moments later, something heavy bumped my left leg! I yelped like a stung puppy! I felt the blood drain from my face. My hair stiffened and a rash of goose bumps galloped up my spine! Terror struck through me! I threw back my arms and kicked back with my legs as hard as I could! I swam backwards as best I could. My float left my grasp! I quickly grabbed it back! I swallowed some water! I was coughing and spluttering and splashing about like a demented fool! I almost went under! I shouted inwardly, 'CALM DOWN, CALM DOWN. PULL YOURSELF TOGETHER MAN!'

Gradually, I slowed down and brought the frantic, aimless swimming to a stop. I gained control of the coughing and spluttering. I made a conscious effort to control my rate of breathing. I began to regain some kind of composure. Then I gasped and grabbed my right thigh! Cramp! The excruciating pain turned my leg into a rigid bunch of knots. 'Bastard, bastard, bastard,' I hissed. Again, I almost lost the now, empty float. I had no choice but to take the pain, tread water as best I could and wait until the agony abated. Gradually, the knots unravelled and the pain eased; As soon as I was able, I refilled the float. Before long, and to my great relief, I settled, the water settled and all was quiet again.

The bout of cramp had taken the edge off my fear of the unknown, but it didn't shift the memory. What had bumped into me? It took a lot of will power to keep my imagination in check. I had to think logically. Naturally, my first thoughts were of some kind of shark. If it was a shark, it seemed to have lost interest, or its' appetite. Then I though perhaps it was a dolphin. Their reputation for curiosity is well known. I was happy with that thought. A large ray perhaps? Could a lump of waterlogged driftwood just beneath the surface be the culprit? I doubted it. After a little more pondering, I settled for a dolphin as being the instigator of my near heart attack and the stupid waist of valuable energy. I tried to put the incident to the back of my boggling mind.

Yet again, I slowly turned and looked about my horizon. Still there was nothing to see or hear. My legs and arms felt heavier. My panicky swim had taken a lot out of them. The inside of my mouth was sticky and tasted foul. In the silence, I could hear my blood being pumped around my aching head. Apart from those minor problems, I was doing ok. Positive thinking. That was the trick. I checked my float. That also was ok. I managed to settle back to steady breathing and treading water at optimum rate. 'It won't be long now sunbeam,' I murmured softly.

The faint sound came from somewhere to my right! I resisted the temptation to make any kind of rash movement. I held my breath and listened. There it was again! The sound of the water rippling! Then, moments later, there came the sound of a soft splash! Somewhere in the darkness, beyond my vision, something was moving about in the water! Once again, I felt the fear grip my heart. This time though, I was determined not to panic. Trying to swim away would be futile and a useless waste of my energy. Slowly, calmly, I turned my body toward where I thought the sounds had emanated. I drew in a deep breath and held it. I stared unblinking into the gloom and listened intently. There it was again, a soft splash followed by a rippling sound! Whatever it was, it was closer now. My body shook with tension. My breathing became fast and jerky. I thought I would choke on my own heart! My whole body went rigid when no more than three or four yards to my front, something quite large broke the surface! The goose bumps made another dash up my backbone. The temptation to make another reckless swim for it was almost overwhelming. Some how though, I managed to keep panic at bay; I steadied myself I slowed my breathing and my movement. Hardly blinking, I stared at the strange, dark object.

The flattish, dome shaped thing wasn't moving. I noticed that there was a similar shaped, but much smaller object six inches or so to the left of the big dome. It soon became apparent that the two objects were part of the same when, quite suddenly, the whole thing turned and came gliding soundlessly towards me! Initially, I was alarmed at its sudden movement. It was obviously a living creature, but what kind? As it approached though, something told me, some instinct or other, that whatever it was, it wasn't dangerous. It seemed to be moving too quietly, too gently to be harmful. Feeling much less apprehensive, I watched in silence as the creature drew near. I was quite taken aback when it slowed, turned slightly and came to a stop a few inches in front of my shaky head. Now that it was right under my nose, the light of recognition dawned; It was an enormous Turtle!

Astonishment, disbelief, relief and elation were among the many emotions I felt at that moment. For fear of frightening it away, I resisted the temptation to laugh out loudly and give the magnificent creature a welcoming slap on its' back. I chuckled softly when it occurred to me that, why this wonderful animal, completely at home in its' natural environment, should be afraid of a stupid, clumsy creature that is completely and literally out of its depth; 'Hello big fellah, pleased to make your acquaintance.' I whispered nervously.

My newfound friend was lying lengthways a few inches in front of me. It was about five and a half feet from its' nose to the rear of its' shell. The shell was dark, the colour of which I couldn't make out in the poor light of the waning moon. It was segmented into plates that were roughly pentagon shaped. Each plate was defined by shallow, lighter coloured grooves. The flesh of the short, thick neck was creased and looked leathery. The reptilian head was aquiline in shape and appeared yellowish with a mosaic pattern of dark, pentagon shapes on top of the head and along the sides of the beak shaped mouth. The eyes were large, dark and seemed expressionless. Some kind of membrane flicked over them like a thin eyelid. I could just make out the shape of the flippers under the water. They looked disproportionately large. They were obviously very efficient.

My float needed a refill. I didn't care. I would have to work harder at treading water for the time being. I didn't want to disturb my bold, friendly new acquaintance. I looked about me, that is, 'us'. I thought perhaps the turtle was not alone. There was no sign of another. I kept my movements to a minimum and breathed as quietly as I could. The beautiful animal floated without effort. The water surrounding it was still. The sound of my movements seemed deafening in the clammy silence. I gazed in wonder at the great creature. I speculated as to weather it was male or female. For some inexplicable reason I concluded that it was female, and that she was making her way to some distant shore in order to lay her eggs. If that was the case, she didn't seem to be in much of a hurry. 'Maybe you've just stopped for a rest old girl'. I whispered. Then I thought that perhaps she was just plain curious and I wondered if she was looking at me with the same sense of wonder that that I looked upon her. I liked the thought, but I doubted it. I considered the odds against such a bizarre encounter. They must have been phenomenal. I didn't care much, I was just grateful of the company; I longed to reach out and run a hand along the length of her gleaming shell. I dared not for fear of alarming her. I longed to let her know that I would do nothing to harm her. It would have been wonderful to.be able to communicate with the silent, friendly ocean going tortoise. Somehow, I felt that she understood my predicament and was sympathetic. I found myself willing her not to leave me; Together, we drifted in the empty, lonely silence. I drew great comfort from being in the presence of such a strong, yet gentle creature. I felt lifted.

My heart sank like a stone when the great amphibian swept her powerful front flippers backwards and glided slowly away from me. A lump filled my throat. I don't know what I expected of the animal, but I was appalled at the prospect of being left alone again. I softly pleaded. 'Oh no, no, please don't go yet, please don't leave me.' She began circling me. I deluded myself into thinking she had heard my pathetic plea. I turned my body so as to keep her in sight. After several circuits, she turned toward me and came in close again. I was overjoyed! 'That's my girl, that's my bonnie lass,' I blurted. I had to gag back the emotion. Once again, we were quietly drifting and again, I felt a comfortable sense of security.

There hadn't been many times in my life when I had felt envious of anything or anybody. At that time though, as I gazed at the free-floating turtle, I felt envious. I envied her effortless swimming ability and her freedom to roam the open sea without restriction. I envied her independence and the apparent simplicity of her life. All she had to do was to survive. If she didn't, who would know? Who would care? Who would shed a tear at the demise of such a creature?

I looked into the eyes of the turtle. I could see no sign of any kind of emotion. The membrane flicked across the shiny orbs and bubbles of mucus emitted from the beaky mouth. Despite my efforts to resist, I ran my hands along the length of the glistening shell. There was no reaction. The next move I made was a foolish one. Gently, very gently, I placed my arms across the width of the creatures' shell. She didn't react. Slowly, carefully, I allowed my weight to ease down onto the Turtle. I relaxed completely. She now had all of my weight; for a few seconds she made no move. For those few seconds I was able to relax completely. It felt wonderful. No, exquisite would be a better description of how much relief I felt in my aching joints and muscles. However, my ecstasy was short lived.

With one majestic sweep of her wonderfully efficient flippers, the noble Lady disappeared from beneath me.

Despite the sudden movement of the Turtle, I managed to react fairly quickly. I didn't go under too far. I got back to the surface quickly and immediately refilled my float with air. Filling the float took a lot out of me. My breathing was laboured. My legs and arms felt cumbersome; what a fool I had been and worse still, I had been an arrogant fool. Because of my arrogance, I was alone again. I had got it into my stupid head that the magnificent, noble Turtle would support me for a while so that I could get some rest. I giggled stupidly, nervously and said. 'Who the hell do you think you are?' What the fuck did you think you were doing?' 'What makes you think that that lovely creature would want a bloody fool like you riding on its' back?' I then shouted. 'SERVES YOU RIGHT IF SHE NEVER COMES BACK YOU PRICK!'

I forced myself to calm down. I looked all around me for a sign of the Turtle. I strained my eyes in the gloom. I hoped upon hope that she would return. Once again I heard myself pleading for her to come back. She did not. The despair and the fear of being alone again took over my senses and filled my heart. Soon, my wretched body was shaking with pathetic, sobbing self-pity. The deep-seated doubt that I would ever see the friendly faces of my shipmates again leapt to the fore. The gut wrenching feeling of complete loneliness swept over me. I felt sick. The absolute silence and the feeling of abandonment, was appalling. 'Why couldn't you leave her be, why for Christ sake' I whimpered.

In the brief time that I had been in contact with the Turtle I had actually formed some kind of bond with her. Stupidly, I felt that we had something in common, us being alone out there. She had become a companion, something for me to believe in, to hang on to. She had been a great comfort to me. When she left me, I felt that she had deserted me. Silly really and perhaps sounding far fetched, but that's how I felt and that feeling deepened my feelings of despair.

I felt so, so tired. My uplifting encounter with the bold Turtle was a drain on my strength. Ad to that the mental strain of extreme nervous tension and the constant presence of my old adversaries, fear and loneliness, I was in a pretty bad way. All of my optimism and the strength boosting of my positive thinking had dwindled. I no longer cared what was to become of me; I drifted in the quiet darkness. I never even bothered scanning the horizon. I closed my tired, tear-filled eyes. I thought of home. I thought of death.

Time had stood still for me. I was treading water and re-inflating the float instinctively. Filling the float was becoming a painful task. Some times, I could only get it half full, even less. I didn't care. I was just doing it because it was the thing to do. I kept my eyes closed as much as possible. I tried to blot everything out of my mind. It was impossible. Hundreds of different, unrelated thoughts raced madly in and out of my confused grey matter. Was I going Mad? It felt like it. More and more thoughts bombarded my fevered brain. Faster and faster they came and went. Names, faces and places. Numbers and colours Bright flashing colours intermingling and forming an unrecognisable smear. Then came the noises. Rhythmic, undulating, eerie noises I was going mad, I was sure of it. I felt that my head was about to burst and my feeble brain be scattered over the surface of the sea.

I completely snapped. I screamed! I screamed the scream of a Madman. I opened my eyes and looked to the sky. I pleaded, yelling as loudly as I could. 'HELP ME? PLEASE, PLEASE HELP ME?' with that, I raised my arms and shook my fists at the heavens and then brought them down hard onto the surface making a loud smacking sound. The sea was unforgiving. My flesh was already tender and sore. The pain caused me to gasp hoarsely. The desperate, maniacal outburst was of course pointless and energy draining. However, it did serve to clear my head a little, because a few moments later I spotted an arc of white light in the far distance.

I stared at the light through blurry, sore eyes. I re-inflated the float. I inflated it by way of a different method this time. Instead of hauling the trousers over my head, I raised them in front of me and brought them down as quickly as possible to the sea surface. This method was less efficient at trapping air but it required much less effort; whilst carrying out. the task, I kept my eyes on the light. My emotions were, to say the least, mixed.

I wanted to believe that the light was emanating from my ship, or indeed any ship. I wanted to believe that the arc of light was the effect of searchlights reflecting their light off the sea in order to find me. But now, deep-seated despondency made it almost impossible for me to put any faith in those beliefs. I didn't know what to believe. I felt calm and resigned as I watched the light. I trod water, I breathed easily, though very noisily now. I closed my eyes again. I felt light headed, almost giddy. The rhythmic throbbing sound was back. It was accompanied by another sound. It resembled the sound of a locomotive steaming away in the distance. They were pleasant, soothing sounds. They helped me to relax. I slept; I couldn't have been asleep for long. My float was still fairly well inflated. What woke me was a familiar sensation and it turned my stomach over.

I was being lifted up on a long, low rolling wave. The roller was followed by another and then another. A long, lazy swell was running. I managed to keep my stomach under control, not that there was anything in it to puke up! I took advantage of the extra height the top of the waves offered and took a good look around my now, slightly more distant horizon. The arc of light was still there. It was impossible to make out if it was moving. Still feeling queasy, I continued scanning the ocean surface. A glimmer of hope was beginning to reinstate itself within me. I was looking for any vessel, one that might have joined in the search. There was no sign of any other navigation lights or searchlights. There was however, a brightening of the sky to the east. The sun was on its way up.

I sighed. It was a deep shuddering sigh. I felt the despondency loosening its demoralising grip. I murmured softly. 'Onward and upwards dear boy, onward and upwards;' I re-inflated my float with determination. Then I set about the task of again, sorting myself out mentally and checking my physical condition. I new my mental state was poor. The encounter with the Turtle helped lift my spirits but in that short time I had become all but obsessed with the creature, so that when it inevitably went on its way leaving me on my own, well, my emotions, already weakened by constant fear and loneliness, got the better of me in a devastating way. I had been weak and foolish. At that point in my thinking I told myself not to dwell upon the subject anymore and to put it out of my mind. I wasn't fairing too well physically either. My joints throbbed, as did my head. My ears sang constantly and I could hear my blood thudding past them. Sharp pains stabbed through my guts intermittently and without warning. Each breath I took made a loud rasping noise and was painful to take. My mouth and throat were parched. The taste in my mouth was disgusting. I knew that I had absolutely no alternative but to put up with all the discomfort, I had no choice and had to resign my self to that fact. The temptation to take even the smallest sip of seawater was strengthening. 'No never!' I hissed.

As the sun rose, my spirits also rose. I harked back to the promise I had made to myself, and my shipmates. "I would do my best to stay alive as long as was possible." I made a concerted mental effort to put all that had happened in the last few hours out of my mind and to have more faith in the possibility of being rescued. 'Onwards and upwards dear boy.' I repeated.

With the absence of clouds, the sunrise was not nearly as spectacular as some I had witnessed in my seafaring time. As always, the sun came up deceptively fast. I watched through squinting eyes as the marigold yellow orb raised itself majestically over the horizon. It wouldn't be long before its' heat would began evaporating some of the moisture in the air and its' diffusing beams turned the atmosphere into a pale blue haze. As the sun got higher the temperature would soar. I would have to take great care not to become too exposed to the celestial inferno. I already had that potentially deadly occurrence covered. I would simply use my number eight-shirt as a sunshade for my head and shoulders. All I had to do was to keep the shirt moist. With the satisfaction of having that problem solved; for the umpteenth time, I refilled my trousers with air. I felt a little more uplifted.

I looked up at the sky. All but the brightest of the stars had faded away in the heartening dawn light. All that was left of the moon was a sliver of a slightly tilted crescent of pale silver. The royal blue of the sky to the west was rapidly giving way to a hazy, sea-blue blanket as it swept across the heavens from the east. I scanned the horizon, concentrating on the approximate area where I had last sighted the arc of man-made light. There was no sign of it. I sighed deeply and shrugged my shoulders. I began thinking. I began to think constructively.

Thankfully, my stomach had settled down a good bit. Now, riding the long, languid swell was much less uncomfortable; I estimated the time of the appearance of the suns' light at about 0300 to 0330 hrs. I reckoned I had been in the water for around three to three and a half hours. Naturally, it seemed a whole lot longer. Official sunrise in that part of the world at that time of year was not long off. By that time I would have been adrift for more than four hours. Four hours didn't sound very long, but four hours of treading water, repeatedly re-inflating the float, the constant turmoil of my emotions and the ever present fear of sudden death, no matter how much it was suppressed, was a wearing and painful drain on my physical and emotional strength. I whispered with as much conviction as I could muster, 'keep going sailor, just keep going and you'll make it! '

With my mind reset and my emotions more in control, I stoically rode the gentle ocean swell and went about the business of keeping my mind occupied. This I did by trying to remember all sorts of different facts and figures that I had learned, or had just picked up over time. Trivia, like the names of famous, and or important people, significant dates and occurrences in history, the names of countries, cities and towns where important events had taken place. I visualised some of the beautiful places I had visited in my travels. I pictured the faces of some of the people I had met in my lifetime I tried to put names to the faces. I tried to remember where it was that I met those people and in what circumstances. My next train of thought was of some of the books I had read and some of the films I had seen. I decided to do a critical revue of them and perhaps even a comparison; My thought process ceased abruptly and my mind cleared instantly when I caught sight of a movement in the periphery vision of my left eye.

Fifteen yards or so to my left dozens of flying fish erupted from the wall of the swell and became airborne. I gasped at the sudden burst of activity. My eyes followed the flight path of the remarkably adapted fish as they skimmed the smooth, shiny tops of the rollers. Their sleek, silver and steel blue bodies gleamed and flashed in the brightening sunshine. As they glided swiftly over the waves, they would occasionally flick the crests with their tail fins. This left behind a random pattern of frothy eddies which slid slowly down into the trough of the swell. The extraordinary fish varied in size from that of a mackerel up to a small to medium sized codfish. I felt slightly disappointed when the glistening creatures folded their wing-like pectoral fins and arrowed, with hardly a splash, back into the waves. They had covered about sixty feet through the air. That was by no means a great distance for the phenomenal fish. I watched beyond the spot where they went back into the water. A little further from that point, the fish took to the air again. This time their glide was shorter. I looked out for them for a while, but they never showed again. Like most seamen, I had observed flying fish on numerous occasions. Every time I saw them, I was always bewitched and highly impressed by their wonderfully adapted airborne skills.

Despite being momentarily distracted from my dilemma by the exciting display by the flying fish and, despite feeling disappointed at their departure, I was relieved that they were heading away from me. Lurking in the back of my mind was the unnerving knowledge that flying fish do not take to the air just for the fun of it. They only break out of their natural environment in order to confuse predators and baffle any attempts to catch and devour them. Like me the flying fish had many sea born enemies. Unlike me, the flying fish were well adapted to make good an escape. My float needed refilling. I could afford to wait a while. My rate of treading water had instinctively slowed.

The sun climbed inevitably higher. The temperature rose and the moisture in the air was noticeably less. It was going to be a very hot day, just like yesterday and no doubt, it would be the same tomorrow. I asked myself, would there be a tomorrow? I cautioned myself sharply, 'don't start thinking like that you fool!' Before long it was light enough for me to be able to make out a more distant horizon. I worked on trying to relax a little more. I tried to resume thinking about anything and everything I could remember in order to take my mind off of my situation. I found it difficult to get a solid chain of thoughts together.

The pain in my joints and aching fatigue were a constant reminder of my plight. Try as I might, the sickly feeling of dread would come over me in demoralising waves.

The familiar rhythmic throbbing sound and the sound of the locomotive was back. I knew that the sounds were not just in my head. I knew that they were the sounds of a ship steaming slowly along not all that far away from me. However, something in my psyche would not allow me to become excited at the fact that there was a ship nearby and that there was a chance of rescue. Methodically, I re-inflated the float as best I could. Inevitably, each effort was decidedly more painful and tiring than the last. Then, with a casual air I waited until I was at the top of a roller until I scanned the horizon; There was nothing to see. I wasn't disappointed. The throbbing sound faded and the loco pulled away into the distance. I emptied my head of all thoughts. Then I filled it with the names of rock-bands. Singers, hit records, musicians etc, etc, etc.

I must have been in some kind of stupor, and for quite some time; I was brought out of it by the foul taste of salt water when it filled my gaping mouth. I spat and spluttered. Luckily, although I was seriously tempted, I didn't swallow any of the stuff. My float was all but devoid of air. I inflated it again. I couldn't get as much air into it as I would have liked. The physical effort required to fill the float would soon be beyond my capabilities. The pain in my joints was becoming barely tolerable. Any extra movement was close to agony. I looked toward the sun. It was at a height in the sky that told me that the time was about 0630 hours. I decided that it would be a good idea to take my shirt off and cover my head. The temperature would soon rise more quickly and there was no shade where I was. In my present condition, even a short period of exposure to the suns' uncompromising rays would not, to say the least, help my situation. If I were to become stupefied again, well, I knew what the consequences could be. I was quite surprised that I was able to think as clearly as I was. I wondered how much longer I would be capable of doing so. With that thought in mind, I went about the business of removing my shirt. It proved to be an extremely painful process. I winced and moaned at each simple, every day move. Even the joints in my fingers seemed to be on fire. I was by now badly dehydrated. The removal of the shirt took a lot out of me. My breathing sounded inordinately loud and now that I was almost completely naked, I felt more vulnerable than ever. I relied on the float for rest as much as I dared. I concentrated on closing my eyes for measured lengths of time, no more than a slow count of twenty. I worked on controlling my rasping, gravely breathing. In one two three, out one two three, in one two three and so on.

Even though my ears seemed to be singing in a higher note, I heard the rhythmic throbbing of engines above it. There was a ship somewhere in my vicinity. I grinned, the muscles in my neck and jaw quivered painfully. Was there a chance? The question stuck in my mind. I dared not think about the answer. I put the thought out of my mind before I got my hopes too high. As I rode the rollers I noticed that there was something different going on. Quite a few minutes passed before I realised that the swell was running higher and the distance between each wave was shorter. There was still not the slightest movement of the air. At the top of each roller I turned as far as I could before descending into the troughs so that I could take a look around. I had to turn very slowly and carefully. Moving in a circle was now torturously difficult. My spine and hips were now full-blooded members of the pain gang. There was more torture when I struggled to re-inflate the float, more still when I soaked my shirt-cum-head shade. The heat of the sun had increased noticeably. The haze had gone from the atmosphere. The sky was totally cloud free. The throbbing of ships' engines was growing in volume. I rested as best I could. I was still afraid to get ebullient over the possibility of being found. I tried some more mind games. Counting backwards from a thousand or saying the alphabet backwards at speed, are two of the many ploys that I tried in order to keep my mind off of certain subjects.

The sound of engines grew louder still. Although I knew it would cause me great pain and would be a drain on my perilously low level of energy, I simply had to have another scan round. As before, I waited until I was at the top of a roller before I started turning. I had only turned a few degrees when I spotted something. Something man-made! It was the slightest of glimpses, but I was certain I saw something! I drifted down the wave. I couldn't wait to get to the top of the next one. I had to resist the temptation to try to swim up the roller. There it was again! It was the top half of the huge, long-range radar scanner in service in the R.N. It must have been the Tern! I strained my neck to keep the 'bedstead,' as it was known, in sight as I descended the wave. I could no longer keep my excitement under control. Positive hope of survival sprang to the fore. As soon as I reached the top of the next roller, ignoring searing pain, I began feebly waving my arms about and made pathetic attempts at calling out.

I winced and gasped hoarsely when I felt the first sting! Another sting followed moments later. Then another! I lost count after about ten stings. I soon realised to my horror that I had drifted into a shoal of jellyfish. In ordinary circumstances, a sting or two from most types of jellyfish are no more harmful than a wasp sting, painful, but normally harmless. My circumstances couldn't be further from normal. With my flesh being so tender and sore from being immersed in salt water for so long, the pain of each sting was excruciating. Add to that, the terrifying thought that there could be among the less harmful jellyfish one or two that are known to be deadly. Panic took hold. Shock bolstered adrenalin surged through my veins and boosted me into mad action. I flailed the water all around me! Again and again the vicious tentacles laid into my thrashing body! I tried to rub the agony out of my burning flesh! I went under! I opened my eyes momentarily. There were jellyfish all around, a myriad of beautiful colours! Instinctively I covered my genitals! I swallowed a great gulp of water! I gagged and choked! My throat was on fire! I was sinking! I grabbed blindly for my float! It was gone! I opened my eyes again. In that instant I saw the colour purple just before I took the sting in my right eye! The pain was indescribable. I thought my eye had exploded! I grabbed my head with both hands and twisted it from side to side! I sank deeper! I reckoned it was all over for me.

My head throbbed. My whole body seemed to be shuddering. A multi coloured, swirling mist formed behind my eyes. Mercifully, all of my pain and discomfort began to ease. Miraculously, my mind became clear. I felt at ease, comforted. Then I smiled when I saw in the distance a familiar, friendly shape. It was the Turtle. She had come to meet me.

There was to be no peace for me though. Something grabbed me by both arms! I didn't feel any real pain. It just felt as though my whole body was one big, dull, ache! I felt myself being dragged along. I had neither the strength nor the will to resist. I felt something hard hit my back and legs I heard strange noises. I heard a voice! It said. 'He's still alive, we'll have to get him back to the ship fast though!'

About 22 hours later, I came too in the two berth sick bay on board H.M.S. Tern. Thanks to the expert care of Leading Medical Assistant 'Pincher' Martin, I quickly recovered from my awful ordeal. Pincher told me about my rescue. Apparently, a member of the sonar listening crew picked up my noises of panic in his headset. He reported the strange noises and the estimated direction they were coming from to the 'ops room. I owed that astute operator a great deal. Fortunately for me, the ship didn't have far to steam before I was spotted going under by an equally astute lookout. Another great debt owed. I was dragged from the ocean by the duty, sea boats crew. The voice was that of Petty Officer Graham. To this day I can still hear his urgent tones. After a few days L.M.A. Martin booted me out of the sick bay. Naturally, I received merciless ribbing. Quips like, 'should have thrown the shrimp back' and 'who gave you permission go swimming' and many more besides were in abundance. I took them, all with a smile and was glad to. I owed my life to every Man on that ship and if ever I mentioned that solid fact, I was told, 'stow it, you would have done the same' I liked to think that would be the case.

Owen Morris came down to my mess-deck after completing his stint in the wheelhouse an hour after I got out of sick-bay. He carried in his arms a set of faded number eights. I looked from his big ruddy face to the clothes and back again. He swallowed hard and said. 'They're yours boyo, I've fixed them up for you.' Then he looked deep into my eyes and choking back tears, he whispered, 'I aint got the words brother.' I stepped forward and embraced the big Welshman. I felt his huge shoulders shudder when I replied with a big lump in my throat. 'Me neither taffy, me neither.'

END

'What the day may bring is a tale of fate. When we each start our day, we have no idea what fate may throw up for us. In the case of the two young boys who are the main characters of this short story, fate dished them up a day of extraordinary events.'

I hope readers will enjoy the tale. I also hope that fate is kind to them.

,   D A Grieve

What The Day May Bring

The warming, sunny July, morning in 1948 had started well for two good friends. Ten year olds Jimmy Green and Peter Brown were to meet up at their usual place which was the bricked up entrance of an air raid shelter. The shelter was one of five world war two communal air raid shelters that had been built in the grounds of a two-story block of maisonettes. The concrete, grass-covered shelters were built in order to accommodate, not only the residents of the maisonettes, but also the workers from the neighbouring factories, warehouses and offices in the event of an air raid.

The boys had lived in the red bricked, shabby looking maisonettes since their birth and had been pals for as long as they could remember. They came from similar working class backgrounds. To a degree, they were similar in appearance. They were thin and wiry, usually grubby and generally unkempt. For most of the summer season, their knees and elbows sported a scab or two. At that point, chalk and cheese came into play and the similarities ended. Jimmy had dark, curly hair that, thanks to the infamous, short back and sides style of haircut, sat on top of his head as though it had been stuck there as an afterthought. He was the more swarthy of the two and his features were sharp. His hazel-green eyes were set deep in their sockets which gave the boy a look of secretive guilt. He was an excitable lad and could at times become aggressive and confrontational. He was known as quite a scrapper among his peers; Peter was a different kettle of fish. His hair was longish and fair and seemed to have a mind of it's own. His skin was also fair. His features were broad, pale and open which gave him the look of honesty and innocence. He was the calmer of the two friends He would think before he leapt, as it were. It seemed almost impossible to rattle him. Jim had long since given up trying.

The lads wore similar clothes. For the sake of economy the clothes were hard wearing and made to last. During the summer months they wore khaki shorts, colourful cotton tee-shirts, that for some obscure reason, were known as 'sloppy-Joes.' On their feet they wore either plimsolls or sandals. Except for school days, socks were never worn on warm summer days.

Both of the boys had numerous sisters and brothers, all of whom, they did their utmost to avoid whenever and wherever they could. They were fortunate in as much as they were allowed a fair degree of freedom to wander about the local area without supervision. This was mainly due to their parents having to work long hours in order to make ends meet. They had to put a lot of trust in their kids. However, from time to time Jimmy and Peter's wanderings were curtailed due to their natural boisterous and mischievous nature leading them into trouble. The boys shared a certain notoriety around the small town of Brenton, which was on the outskirts of London. Some local people considered them to be tearaways. Most folks however, kept in mind the meaning of the adage. 'Boys will be boys.'

The two friends were well aware of the consequences of getting into any kind of trouble more serious than that of boyish tomfoolery. The fear of serious parental punishment was usually enough to keep the lads on the straight and narrow, especially Jim. His father was in the habit of beating his son severely in the event of him bringing trouble to his door. Young Jim was often the object of derision and physical abuse at the irrational whim of his Father.

Whist out and about, the seemingly, ever presence of the formidable local Bobby, Constable Joyce, also served to keep the boys in check. He was a giant of a man. Standing well over six feet tall and weighing in at around seventeen stones. He was known locally, and with deliberate irony as Tiny Joyce. He was an extremely effective deterrent. As well as him, there were plenty of other deterrents. Ever watchful Aunties, Uncles and nosey neighbours. Also local shopkeepers, park keepers and other figures of authority. All these people had to be watched out for by the lads while they were out and about. The local and extremely efficient grapevine of informants seemed to the lads to be like a group of conspirators that were determined to prevent them from having any kind of fun at all.

Whilst waiting for Jimmy to turn up, Peter was kicking around the scorched and twisted remains of the tail-fin of an incendiary bomb. There were many of these terrible reminders of world war two lying around and about the maisonettes; His ankles were already accumulating a layer of dirt from the powdery dust he was raising; Suddenly and seemingly from nowhere, Jimmy appeared.

'Watcha Pete, how're ya doin?' He gushed brightly causing his pal to start.

'I'm good Jim, are you, ok?' Pete's greeting wasn't as cheery as Jim's. However, he did elaborate it by pulling a ridiculous face, lifting his right knee, clenching his left fist and farting loudly.

In an effort to reciprocate the greeting with a fart of his own, Jim screwed up his face, pushed out his backside and clenching both fists, he tried to force one. He failed. Not to be outdone though, he gulped in a gutful of air and loosed a resounding belch which caused a flock of pigeons to take panicked flight from their roost on the roof of the maisonettes; The lads stood grinning broadly at one and other for a short while.

Jim's nose wrinkled when he caught a nostril full of fart. Pete was already grimacing. Holding their breath, they made their exit from the contaminated area. They hastily walked the few yards to the low, broken down wall that separated the maisonette grounds from the main road that ran through town. The boys sat down on the slightly dew dampened wall.

'You stink rotten!' Exclaimed Pete breathlessly as he gulped fresh air.

'Yea I know, but it was nowhere near as bad as that'n you dropped in the swimming baths that time, I don't think anything'll beat that!'

'Yea, too right. That poor kid swam straight into the bubbles didn't she. I thought she was gonna chuck up!'

'I thought she was gonna bleedin drown!'

The boys laughed heartily as they re-lived getting chucked out of the baths for upsetting the unfortunate girl and being an, "*odorous nuisance*" as old Mother Stevens, the baths supervisor put it; After a short while they settled and sat quietly for a minute or so contemplating what the day may bring.

'Whatr'e we gonna do today then?' Enquired Pete with a sigh.

' I dunno,' said Jim, also sighing.

'What about the cut,' suggested Pete without much enthusiasm.

' No I don't fancy the canal today. We don't need to run into them gits with the air rifles again do we?'

'Na, your right. They nearly got us last time. I can still hear them slugs whislin past me nut!'

'Yea, me too.'

'What about the river?'suggested Pete again.

'Better not, me Uncle Tom's workin his barge down this stretch for all this week and I've been told to stay away from the river cos o that kid drownin last week. If old Tom sees me he's bound to split on me.' Said Jim earnestly.

'Oh; right then,' agreed Pete resignedly.

The lads kicked their heels on the wall while they sat. They were deep in thought. The dew was drying in the still, warming air of the morning. It was very quiet, the only significant sounds were those of a toilet flushing and a baby crying somewhere in the maisonettes; A few minutes later, Pete stopped kicking and slowly stood up.

Softly and with an air conspiracy he said,

'I know what we could do. We could go to that bomb site behind the library and see if we can open that trap door we found in that cellar there the other week, there's gotta be something interesting down there aint there!' Jim's eyes widened and brightened at the sugestion and, punching the air he half shouted, 'Yea, that's a great idea, we cou....'

'What about Tiny though!' Pete interrupted sounding alarmed.

'Oh shit! I forgot about him, he nearly nabbed us last time we was on that site didn't he.'

'Yeah, he did didn't he, the git. But it was a scream when he fell down that hole though weren't it!'

' Yeah, I couldn't run for bleedin laughin. I nearly pissed meself!'

The boys laughed heartily on recalling the vision of Tiny Joyce disappearing behind a mound of rubble when he fell into the cellar; After the laughter had subsided, Jim suddenly stood up and declared loudly,

'I'm goin anyway!' 'All we have to do is keep a good lookout and be as crafty as Hell!'

After thinking for about thirty seconds, Pete agreed and stated defiantly and also loudly,

'You're dead right, lets do it!'

A few moments later, Jim and pete started out on the half mile walk to the bomb site and the half hidden trap-door with who knew what hidden secrets and-or treasures lying below; With it being a Sunday and early in the morning, the main road was almost devoid of motor traffic. There weren't many people about either. The main road, which led to the library and the bomb site, was only wide enough for two lanes of traffic. One for each direction. The pavement on either side of the road was narrow and a lot of the paving slabs were cracked. As they walked along, the lads horsed about, noisily pushing and shoving each other and laughing a lot whilst putting the damaged slabs to use in a boisterous game of broken buscuits.

The road was lined on both sides by an assortment of shops, pubs and offices, none of which opened on Sunday mornings. The only outlet of any interest to the boys was a motorcycle salesroom with a double windowed front. Whenever they passed that way, they would stop admire, and pass comment on what was on offer. After a few minutes of arguing the toss over which bike was the one to buy, they would inevitably agree on the best of all and move on. The game of broken buscuits would be resumed.

A little further along the road, past the rows of shops there was a railway bridge. The slope up and over the bridge was steep. At the foot of both sides of the bridge and on the side of the road that the lads were on, there was a set of huge advertising hoardings. At the rear of the hoardings the ground sloped away steeply and had been planted with a variety of evergreen shrubs. A set of wooden steps led down the slope to a small pathway that led onto a road from the posh end of town. That road also led onto a small railway station. The hoardings were supported by a construction of wooden scaffolding. The main supporting struts of the scaffold were steeply angled and sunk deep into the ground at the foot of the slope. To Jim and Pete, the series of struts, cross-members and braces holding up the hoardings, were an irresistible framework to play about on. The low, steel tubing and concrete posted fencing around the structure was no barrier to the local kids. The easily traversed, horizontal tubing was worn shiny due to the many kids that were drawn to the giant climbing frame. The grass on the mud slope was almost trodden away. Pete and Jim took advantage of the fact that they had the whole thing to themselves.

The framework offered a series of challenges for all who dared them. Pete and Jim were always ready to take on the toughest climbs of the frame. The boys had a good look around about them before nipping behind the hoardings. The coast was clear. There were no nosey parkers around.; Naturaly, being ten year olds, they had vivid and highly active imaginations and a sense of adventure that saw little danger. Now, they were no longer behind the big advertising hoardings. In their minds eye, they were deep in the darkest of dark jungles! They were no longer schoolboys. They were now intrepid explorers on a perilous mission! Now, the shrubs were impossible to penetrate on foot. They were deadly with poisonous thorns and huge, gaping, carnivorous plants that were capable of swallowing a man whole! The shrubs were also teeming with lethal creatures, such as, twenty foot long, poisonous snakes! There were giant spiders with six inch, lethal fangs! Huge Gorillas and ferocious Tigers and Lions lurked! There were also deep, deep chasms and roaring, torrential rivers; Of course, the only way for the explorers to negotiate those deadly obstacles was to climb up and over them via the tall trees.

Jim was the first to set off on the perilous climb into the imaginary jungle canopy. Pete followed close behind.

They grunted, yelled and whooped as they precariously jumped, swung and hopped about on the structure. They encountered and killed many dangerous creatures and had several close calls whilst traversing the chasms and rushing rivers. They were oblivious of any contusions, scratches and grazes they collcted during the adventure; It took all of fifteen minutes or so for the lads to complete the fantastic, exciting journey.

Jim and Pete sat astride the last cross member at the far end of the scafolding structure. Their faces had a bloom of grime that had accumulated over a sheen of sweat. Their chests heaved as their lungs worked to replenish their blood with much needed oxygen. Their faces shone with excitement. They looked into each others eyes. They were smiling brightly, they were too breathless to speak.

'OI, GET DOWN OFF O THERE, AFOR YA BREAK YA BLOODY KNECKS!'

The booming demand was shouted by Mr Ned Graham, the bad tempered and very loud Station Master. He was walking slowly towards the fence bordering the station. He had a cigarette dangling from his lips and a large mug of tea in his right hand. He was gesturing angrily to the boys with his left. He worked every weekend at the station and was known locally as "Noisy Ned". He was called this because apart from being bad tempered, it seemed that he was incapable of talking without shouting; The boys jumped at the sound of his barking, voice. It hadn't occurred to the Man that he could have scared the lads and caused them to fall from their precarious perch. The cross-member they were sitting on was directly over the rusty, old chain-mesh fence that bordered the station.

It was a fair drop! Pete quietly sidled along the cross-member to the front of the hoarding and made his way down to the road-way fence. Jim sat glaring defiantly at the Station master, he didn't like being balled at. The man only had to *tell* them to clear off. There was no need for shouting.

'COME ON, MOVE YA BLOODY SELF BOY!' Yelled Ned slopping his tea carelessly

'ALL RIGHT, ALL RIGHT I'M GOIN AINT I!' Balled Jim defiantly and angrily as he followed Pete.

'DON'T GIMME NO LIP BOY, YOU'LL GET A BLEEDIN CLIP SO YA WILL!'

'OH YEA, YOU'LL HAVE TO CATCH ME FIRST YA MOUTHY OLD GIT!'

'YOU'D BETTER SHUT YA GOB BOY, I KNOW WHO YOU AND THAT OTHER LITTLE BASTARD ARE!' Ned was getting angrier by the second. Jim was equally angry and was ready with his next reply. Pete got in first though.

'ALL RIGHT NED WE'RE GOIN, WE'RE GOIN! He shouted sounding apologetic.

'IT'S MR GRAHAM TO YOU YA LITTLE SHIT, NOW BUGGER OFF THE PAIR OF YA!'

'OH YOU'RE SUCH A GENT MR GRAHAM!' Skitted pete with a posh affectation to his voice. This enraged Noisy Ned.

'BUGGER OFF YA LITTLE BASTARDS! GET AWAY FROM HERE OR I'LL SWING FOR THE PAIR OF YA SO I WILL!' His cigarette flew from his mouth in a spray of brown spit and he spilled most of his tea.

Looking down at Ned from over the road fence, Pete and Jim made some crude gestures and sang out in high pitched, girly voices. 'TA TA FOR NOW NEDDY!'

A string of loud, disgusting expletives followed them as they hopped over the fence and trotted up the slope of the bridge. They cringed as they sniggered.

There were no trains travelling in either direction at that time so the boys didn't bother stopping to climb on to the bridge's parapet to watch them pass under and for the pair to become engulfed in smoky steam. Anyhow, they had had enough of the abusive, Noisy Ned.

On the other side of the bridge and on the opposite side of the road was the local rubbish dump. This was another place at which the boys had spent many happy hours. It was a small patch of hilly land that was boxed in by a row of the back yards of terraced houses to the rear, the railway lines to the right and a small hospice to the left. The front, where the road ran by, was fenced off with the same inadequate type of fencing as was round the hoardings. There was also a line of low, thick shrubs flourishing immediately behind the fence.

The old adage that says, "one man's rubbish is another man's treasure" certainly rang true for Jimmy and Peter. The dump was one of those where only quality rubbish was placed. Stuff like perfectly good clothing, broken furniture, empty boxes, boxes with assorted stuff in them, and the odd bit of intriguingly unrecognisable rubbish. The lads had a secret stash of many treasures they'd found on the dump over time; They crossed the road and as they walked by the dump, the boys discussed whether or not to pay the place a visit. The talking petered out when Pete elbowed Jim sharply in the ribs when he spotted a familiar figure amongst some shrubs in the dump. It was a tall, grey-haired Man. He was a tramp and he was. known as "Posh."

Nobody knew of the tramp's background. He had been turning up in town from time to time over the past few years and was a well known character. Even though he was a tramp, he was trusted and treated with respect by most of the folks of the local community. The reason for their trust was that he once saved the life of a lady that had somehow fallen into the river that flowed around the town. She said that she couldn't remember falling in, only that she thought she had been pushed! Nobody took too much notice of the unfortunate Woman as she was known to be a little dotty. However, not only was she unable to swim, she was weighed down with heavy clothing and a hefty handbag which she clung on to for dear life! Without a second thought, Posh dived in and, swimming against strong tide and undertow, saved the lucky Lady from a watery death.

The rescue was indeed newsworthy, but it was made even more so by the fact that the good lady was the wife of the Mayor. One reporter managed to get a few words from Posh about the incident, but that was all. An article covering the incident appeared in the local rag the next day. However, before any accolades could be bestowed upon Posh, he upped and left town leaving a note pinned to the front door of the Town-Hall explaining that, "it is no more than a man's duty to protect and defend his fellow man." Honouring his obvious wish of anonymity, the matter was pursued no further by the local press or the authorities.

As well as Posh, he was known by several different names. Names such as "The Professor," "The General," "The Aristocrat" and a few others. To the local kids he was known as Posh simply because he had a posh way of talking. All the names were the same to the tramp himself though; His real name however, was known to nobody.

The fact that Posh was at the dump ended any indecision by the boys on whether or not to go onto the dump themselves. Moments later, Pete and Jim were carefully picking their way through various piles of rubbish, small heaps of old masonry and grass tufted mounds of clay etc on their way towards Poshs' camp site. The temperature was rising as the Sun rose higher in the clear morning sky. Shadows lengthened. Flying insects of all kinds were taking to the air from grassy patches and the shrubbery that thrived in the dump. Small birds darted from bush to bush.

As the lads approached Posh he turned to greet them. He was a tall big boned Man. His large head was topped with thick, iron-grey hair that was kept trimmed. His features were rugged and tanned. His blue eyes were set wide in his broad face. He had a prominent, hooked nose. His mouth was wide and thin, his jaw square. His large hands gave the impression of great strength. He was dressed in a suit of threadbare tweeds. His grey flannel shirt was well worn at the collar. His tie was faded but the pattern of angled, blue, red and green stripes were still prominent. His heavy, brown boots were worn but well coated with dubbin. It was difficult for people to understand how and why Posh had become a tramp. Like most tramps he was, to say the least, enigmatic; He recognised Jim and Pete and welcomed them.

'Hello there boys, it's a pleasure to see you both again, especially on such a beautiful morning.' His voice was warm and slightly lilting, his accent was pure Oxford English.

'Hiya Posh,' acknowledged Pete and Jim brightly and almost in unison.

Posh turned his head slightly and peered at the boys out of the corner of a twinkling blue eye and enquired, 'well, what have you young scallywags been up to lately, eh?'

In an attempt to look inocent, Jim open his eyes wide, raised his eyebrows, held his hands wide and replied, 'nothing Posh, nothing at all!'

'Me neither Posh, me neither!' Denied Pete overdoing the innocent inflection in his voice.

'Yes, well, I'll believe you, thousands wouldn't though. Now then chaps, wont you come into my humble, albeit temporary abode so that we can have a little chat?' The invitation was emphasised with a theatrical sweep of his left arm.

The lads didn't need to asked twice. Posh's stories about his adventures and his travels were not to be missed. He was a terrific story teller.

A space between a couple of Elderberry shrubs and a large Buddleia was what served as a camp for the rugged gentleman of the road. The wall of the hospice was twenty yards beyond. A small primus stove standing on a piece of broken paving slab occupied the centre of the space. Posh had already packed most of his belongings away in his, large, ex-military rucksack, other bits and pieces lay round about. An overturned beer crate served as a seat for him; Avoiding the larger, harder of the tufts of rough wild grass, the boys sat down cross legged a yard or so in front of the crate. Posh sat on the crate, placed his elbows on his knees and intertwined his long, thick fingers. He looked keenly through half closed eyes from Pete to Jim.

As he did so he breathed a deep sigh and uttered in low, searching tones.

'Well then, are you going to tell me. What have you two rascals been at eh?' It sounded to the lads like an accusation and they were lost for a reply for a few moments. They sat staring at one and other, there was quite a pause before they could answer; The sound of insects and small birds darting, buzzing and chirping in and around the camp sounded overly loud; Eventually though, Jim inhaled, then exhaled noisily and gave an answer. A barrage of questions of his own immediately followed, taking Posh by surprise.

'We aint bin doin nothing Posh, honest!' He said pointedly. 'Anyway. What *you* bin doin?' 'Where've you been lately?' 'Av ya bin anywhere new?' 'Av ya been on loadsa trains?' 'Av ya been on a ship?' Tell us one of ya stories will ya?' Jims' voice rose in volume as he excitedly blurted out the questions. Pete looked on grinning and nodding enthusiastically.

With pushing gestures of his large hands, Posh held off the torrent of excited questions.

'Whoa lad, whooa, hold your horses for goodness sake, give a chap time to think!' He sounded slightly miffed. He glanced to and fro from Pete and Jim for a few moments. Then he clasped his hands together again and spoke evenly.

'Now then lads, in answer to your questions. Since I was last in this neck-o-the woods I've travelled all over the country. North, South, East and West. Here, there and everywhere. Never remaining in one place for more than a few days at a time. Sometimes even less. I have to say that during my travels nothing much in the nature of adventure or excitement occurred this time round. I have no stories of any real interest to tell. When my business is complete in this town, I shall move on to pastures new once again; Now then chaps, does that answer your questions? Posh sounded inpatient. Bad tempered!

It sounded and felt to Pete and Jim as if they had just been given a statement. The abruptness of Poshs' answer made them feel as if they had been told off! They stared at one and other in silence for a moment. Disappointment showed clearly in their faces for they were expecting to hear stories and descriptions of different and exciting Towns, Cities and even foreign lands.

A disillusioned Jim sighed deeply and started to roughly, uproot the grass from a large tuft in front of him. Pete looked up at Posh and asked softly.

'Didn't you av *any* adventures then Posh?'

'None to speak of old chap.' He sounded less serious.

'Not even anything a little bit exciting?'

'Not really.'

'Oh; right then.' Pete sounded fed up. He also sighed deeply and began tearing at a tuft of grass. There was a minute or so of Quiet before Posh cleared his throat noisily and said. 'Look lads, why don't you tell me about some of *your* adventures? I'm sure you must have something interesting you can tell me about, some secrets you can divulge. like, what will you be getting up to today? Where will you be going? Will you be going anywhere shall we say, *special*?' The latter question was asked in conniving tones.

Jim looked at Posh incredulously. He noticed a certain look in the tramps eyes as he glanced from Pete to himself. It was an odd look. Jim couldn't put his finger on what it meant.; Posh had noticed the look of suspicion in Jim's eyes. Jim cleared his own throat and said 'I dunno, I reckon we'll just have a wander round town and see what there is to do.'

'We was gonna go down the cut or maybe the river,' said Pete casually.

'Well why don't you?' said Posh shortly.

'Well for one thing there's a gang of kids with air guns hangin about the cut these days and they tried to shoot us the last time we bumped into them!' Pete sounded deflated.

'Yea, and my Uncle Tom's working this stretch of the river 'till next week an we aint supposed to bloody-well go near the bloody river!' Jims' voice reflected his bad mood.

'What about the park?' Sugested Posh half heartedly.

'No no, not the rotten park, said Pete quickly. That orrible parkie 'Corkscrew' follows us everywhere we go in his rotten park, we don't get a chance to even *look* in his rotten pond let alone get some rotten sticklebacks! I hate 'im and his rotten park!

'Yeah, me too,' agreed Jim whilst releasing a long, squeaky fart.

Posh looked at Jim, smiled wryly, shook his head and got to his feet. He yawned noisily and stretched his large frame as he made his way out of his camp area. Pete followed close behind. Jim jumped up suddenly with a yelp!

'SHIT, SHIT, DOUBLE SHIT! RED ANTS! I'VE BEEN SAT ON A RED ANTS NEST!'

'Serves ya right for farting on the nest daft arse!' said Pete between guffaws.

Jim cavorted around for a while as he swatted at the stinging insects. His legs soon showed evidence of the bites they had inflicted. Red blotches began to appear among the corpses of the squashed ants. Pete disappeared for a short while but soon returned with a fistfull of Dock-Leaves. Still chuckling, he handed the leaves to Jim. Jim twisted and crushed the leaves to a pulp and fashioned them into a mushy ball. He then rubbed the mush all over the affected areas on his legs. Before long, his thighs were a fetching shade of bright olive green; Shortly, the stinging eased by which time, Jim was completely fed up.

Jim was puzzled by the tramps attitude. He felt as though the usually easy going Posh was after something. He couldn't understand why he was so interested in what he and Pete had been up to and what their plans were for the day. He'd never bothered asking before now. He decided that it was time to get away from Posh for now. He no longer trusted the man. He had the feeling that something was not quite right! He looked around about and caught sight of Posh relieving himself behind a small thicket of shrubs. Time to go, he thought to himself

'Come on Pete, let's go. We'll walk up to the Library and have a look at that bomb site.'

'Yeah, we can av a butchers at that trap-door can't we.' Pete was also ready to leave as he had the feeling that there was something odd about Posh as well.

'See you again sometime Posh.' Said Pete politely as they headed off towards the road at a trot.

'STOP! STAY WHERE YOU ARE! Ordered the tramp sharply. The two friends jumped, stopping in their tracks. Jim grabbed Pete's upper arm. They turned to face Posh.

They didn't like the expression on his face, it un-nerved them. As he strode slowly towards them he clenched and un-clenched his fists. The boys began back peddling. Pete leaned his head in close to Jims

'Did you hear that?' He whispered

'Course I bloody heard him, do'ya think I'm bleedin deaf!' Hissed Jim.

'No, no! Did you hear the funny accent he had when he shouted!' Jim opened his mouth to reply but the long shadow of Posh fell across them. They fell silent. Posh sighed and seemed to relax.

'There's no need to back away lads, I'm not going to hurt you, we're friends aren't we?' He said calmly and condescendingly.

'Why did ya shout like that then?' Demanded Jim, his jaw jutting.

'Yea, why did ya?' reiterated Pete defiantly.

Posh was smiling broadly when he apologised. 'I'm sorry boys, I didn't mean to be so rude. Its just that I didn't want to see you get into trouble or perhaps even, get hurt.'

Jim had an expression of suspicion on his face when he stated. 'Oh yea, how are we gonna get hurt then? How are we gonna get into trouble? We know what we're doin!'

Posh casually waved a hand in the direction of the dump fence which was just a few yards away and suggested, 'look, why don't we have a seat on the fence and I'll explain.'

The boys looked at each other and then looked up into the twinkling blue eyes of the tall tramp. He looked and sounded earnest. Jim released his grip on Pete. Moments later the trio were at the fence. Posh sat sideways on the tubular rail and placing his right hand on the nearby concrete post, he indicated that Pete and Jim should sit on the rail on the other side of the post. The boys complied. Once they were sitting, Posh looked back and forth from one boy to the other for a few moments. He then looked up into the clear, blue sky. It seemed to the boys as though he was looking for some kind of help from above. Pete gave Jim a gentle nudge. They glanced at each other wondering, what now? A train steaming noisily by fifty yards or so behind Posh interrupted the quiet of the still morning. Posh took a deep breath and began talking, evenly and seriously.

'Bomb sites are extremely dangerous places to play around on lads and I wouldn't mind betting that your parents have warned you many times of the dangers of fooling around in such places. In my travels, I've heard many stories and read a lot of reports of children, and indeed grown-ups getting into all sorts of trouble on and around bomb sites and the like. Many children have been seriously hurt and even killed while playing in those places; There was a pause while Posh tried to glean from the looks on the boys' faces whether or not what he was saying was sinking in. He couldn't tell. He breathed another deep breath, folded his arms and continued with his patronizing warning.

'Look lads, I'm the last person on Earth who would want to spoil your fun in any way, I just don't like the idea of either of you getting hurt, or much, much worse, *killed*!' Great emphasis was placed on the word killed and a hint of that strange accent was back. Posh leaned slowly back putting his weight on his other hand. It seemed he had finished his lecture. At least a lecture was what it sounded like to Jim and Pete.

Jim was looking down at some stones he was shoving around with his foot. Pete was staring past Posh, at plumes of steam rising above the hoardings obscuring the station and the train that was stopped there. Both of the lads new that all of what Posh had said was true and made perfect sense. What they couldn't understand though, was why he was talking to them as though they were five year olds? Why was he suddenly so concerned about them? He never had been before! Although they were young and inexperienced, Pete and Jim were not stupid and disliked being taken for stupid. They knew what flannel was when they heard it. They felt belittled, insulted. It seemed to them that Posh had some kind of motive for the warning lecture. Was there something on the site he wanted for himself? Something under that trap-door perhaps!

Jim raised his head, looked into Posh's eyes and asked the questions that were also on Pete's lips. 'What do you care what we do and where we go? Your not my Mum. What's it got to do with you?' 'What's so special about *that* bombsite?'

Pete chimed in defiantly. 'Yeah, we can do anything we want and go anywhere we like, you don't even live round here, why should *you* be bovered?'

At that, Posh stood slowly up and stared hard at the pair. His whole demeanour changed. Somehow he looked bigger. His posture was threatening. His hands became huge fists, the knuckles showed white. His warm, bright blue eyes had narrowed and turned to shards of ice. He leaned over until his face was within inches of the boys and glancing from one to the other he uttered in a guttural, and now heavily accented, menacing, voice. 'Now then. The pair of you will listen to me very carefully! I've tried to warn you off in the nicest way I could. However, it's obvious that you have not listened to a word I have said! Be that as it may, you *will* listen to what I say now! If I see either of you on or anywhere near that bomb site again you'll both be very, very sorry! You two have made me extremely angry! I don't like being made angry, especially by a couple of silly kids! Now then! Have I made myself clear?' The words of the last setence were drawn out very slowly and sounded menacing, threatening. The look in the tramps' eyes was that of dreadful evil!

Jim and Pete were transfixed. Jim managed to put on a look of pure, defiant contempt. He looked into the icy eyes pretending to be unafraid; Suddenly, Posh slapped Jim across the face. Then, without another word he straightened up, turned on his heels and headed back to his camp. A tear ran down Jims' reddening cheek. It was a tear induced by anger and humiliation rather than pain. He felt hatred fill his heart; The lads remained sitting for a while. They were lost for words. Posh had scared them! Pete was the first to suggest leaving.

'Come on Jim, lets get out of ere, lets go before he comes back this way!'

'Yea, yea, ok! But I won't forget that Pete, I won't forget that!' Uttered Jim shakily.

The boys set off walking back towards the railway station. After a few yards their walk speeded up. A few more yards and they were running. They ran almost all the way home. They came to a halt at the broken wall in front of their meeting place. Breathlessly, they looked back in the direction of the railway bridge. There was no sign of Posh; Moments later, when they had regained normal breathing, Pete and Jim sat down on the wall. They sat quietly for a few minutes avoiding eye contact. Jim felt ashamed and was sure Pete felt the same. Ashamed for being scared and ashamed for running away. There was a lot of tension in the air around them. Jim broke that tension. Suddenly, he grabbed up a handy sized piece of broken wall, stood up and hurled it across the road. It hit an advertising hoarding that was fixed to the wall alongside a tobacconist shop. It hit hard and left a deep gouge in the colourful picture. He stood staring at his pointless handy-work. He clenched his fists tightly, he was shaking with rage. Through clenched teeth he snarled. 'Fuck im! Fuck that bastard! He can't tell me what to do! I'll go anywhere I want and do anything I want! Bollocks to im!'

Pete had seen Jim in a rage before. He was wise enough to keep his mouth shut untill his pals' anger had subsided; Pete also felt angry about what had happened and what had been said by Posh. It wasn't so much what Posh had said, it was the way in which he said it. He was the last person on Earth that the lads thought would talk down to them. They were always glad to see the man and so were many other kids in the area. He was always ready with stories of his travels. It was true that some of them sounded a little far fetched but who cared, they were always highly entertaining. He was always good fun to be with. Well he used to be! Posh was always a bit on the nosey side. He was always asking questions about what had been going on in and around town in his absence. Never though, had he been so inquisitive as to what Pete and Jim had been up to, or indeed, what they were going to be *getting* up to. It then occurred to Pete, that Posh often asked if Tiny Joyce was still walking the beat locally. The boys assumed that Posh was a friend of the big Bobby. I wonder, thought Pete? Also, where did the strange accent come from?

After a while, Pete sensed that Jim had calmed down. He glanced at him, and then at the hoarding across the road. 'Did you aim for that spot?' He asked casually.

Jim looked across at the hoarding. 'course I did.' He said flatly.

'Well, it was a bleedin good shot I must say, right in the goolies!'

The hoarding advertised an American brand of hand rolling tobacco. It consisted of a colourful picture of Cowboy on a western ranch leaning on a corral fence busily rolling a cigarette. Jim, proving his renowned reputation among his peers for his powerful and accurate stone-throwing skills, had indeed hit what he was aiming for. The piece of wall had hit the smiling Cowboy solidly in the testicles!

There was still anger in Jims voice when he barked. 'Yea, well, I was thinking of that git Posh when I chucked that stone!'

'Well I'm glad I wasn't on the receiving end of it, it would have make me eyes water and that's no error!' Pete was trying to soften Jims' mood.

With a deep shuddering sigh, Jim turned and looked at his pal saying wistfully. 'Aint you even a little bit mad at that big shit?'

'Course I am! I feel like chuckin a stone at im just like you, but you know I couldn't hit a cows' arse with a cricket bat at point blank range!' Pete noticed the trace of a smile appear on Jims' face.

'Yeah, but you don't even *sound* mad Pete.'

Pete arched his eyebrows, opened his eyes wide and stated 'I'm mad alright Jim, I'm just not as barmy as you are!'

The boys stood looking at each other in silence for a while. Pete was grinning warmly. Moments later, Jim was also smiling. Pete threw a soft punch at Jim which was blocked with much practiced ease. Jim threw one back. Pete tried to step back out of reach. The back of his legs came up against the wall and he pitched backwards over it and landed, with a yelp, on his back. His feet and arms were pointing straight upwards at the sky.

Jim began chuckling as he watched his pal struggling to get up from his awkward position. Pete grunted and groaned. During the struggle he farted loudly; It was some time before the pair recovered from their fits of laughter.

Once they had calmed down, The boys sat down on the wall again; Again, they sat in silence for a while. They listened to the sound of cars and lorries on the airport road a quarter of a mile distant. They watched as cars and bicycles passed to and fro in front of them along he road through town. The place was waking up.

A police car with four officers on board, two in plain clothes, passed rapidly by travelling in the direction of the library. Ten seconds later, another big, black Wolsey was driven by in the same direction. It also had four coppers in it. Pete and Jim stood up and watched as the cars drove out of sight over the railway bridge. Something unusual was happening. The lads had never seen that amount of Policemen all at one time before, *and* in squad cars!

Jim said excitedly, 'come on Pete, lets see if we can find out what's happenin!'

Pete was taken by surprise. 'Eh? What? Oh, right, I'm commin.' He soon caught up with Jim, who was already running towards the bridge.

On reaching the slope of the bridge Pete queried breathlessly. 'What about Posh?'

'We'll keep a sharp look-out, I aint worried about that git! Stated Jim confidently.

They came to a halt at the top of the bridge and looked down the road as far as the bend to the right beyond which stood the library three hundred yards or so distant. There was no sign of the squad cars. The boys turned their attention to the gap in the fence that led on to the dump. They watched for a short while before Jim, with a nod of his head, whispered, 'lets cross the road Pete.'

Once on the other side of the road the boys ducked down below the hight of the bridge parapet and slowly, quietly crept down the slope towards the dump fence. On reaching the start of the fence, they stopped and Jim carefully reached into the shrubs behind the fence in an effort to clear a gap to see through. Despite being blooded several times by long, sharp thorns, he managed to clear a pretty fair viewing gap. He was taken aback by what he saw.

'Blimey Pete, av a look at this!' He whispered hoarsely.

'What? What's up?' Hissed Pete as he siddled up to Jim.

'Coppers, and they're poking round Poshs' camp and searchin his gear!'

In an attempt to get a better view, Pete shoved his arm through the shubbs alongside Jims' arm. He also got pricked. 'Bollocks he rasped!' His pain was soon forgotten when he saw the coppers.

'Bloody ell, what the bloody ell are they lookin for? What d'ya think Posh has been up to?'

'No idea Pete. Posh can't be there though, and I wouldn't mind listsenin to what them coppers are talking about.' They were too far away to make out the Policemen's words.

'Me to, c'mon Jim!' This time it was Pete that dashed off. Jim quickly followed.

Pete led them past the dump and down a set of well-worn, stone steps that led onto the grounds of the tiny Hospice situated at the side of the dump. A solidly built, five foot, sandstone wall separated the Hospice grounds from the dump. There was a narrow, neatly trimmed border of lawn-grass running the length of the wall; To the lads, the Hospice was a place of mistery. It was a long, low, sandstone building with a flat roof. There was a narrow, tarmac drive-way sloping down from a small junction at the main road at the bottom of the railway bridge. The road was bordered on both sides by well tended flower beds. It appeared that the only way in or out of the building was through a wide set of double doors that were heavily ornate with metal studding and strapping. There were few windows and what there were of them were small with tiny pains and the dark curtains were rarely, if ever, drawn open. The Hospice was run by Nuns. Under normal circumstances, the boys would keep well clear of the place. To Pete and Jim, the Nuns were even more of a mystery than the Hospice. If they would but admit it, they were a little afraid of them.

The boys managed to reach the Hospice wall without being spotted by the Bobbys. They were a little breathless but managed to keep the noise of their breathing to a minimum. They crouched at the foot of the wall and listened intently. It was difficult to make any sense of what the Policemen were saying at first, for they were still a fair distance away. As luck would have it though, the Policemen moved closer to the wall and could be heard lighting up cigarettes. Now their voices could be clearly heard by the young eavesdroppers.

It soon became apparent that Posh was a complete fraud. His life as a tramp was no more than a masquerade. He was in fact a German and his real name was Herman Getz; During the war, he was the director of a group of British, Nazi sympathisers and propagandists that were based at various locations throughout the UK. Travelling under cover to and from the continent, it was his job to supply his group members with information, money, equipment, their tasks and just about anything else they would need to discretely spread anti-British proper gander, political unrest and generally help throw spanners into the works of the British war machine.

His reason for being in Brenton was because one of his operators was an employee of the local Library. Conveniently, this man had lived in a small house at the rear of the library. Inconveniently for him however, the house was demolished by the blast from a large bomb dropped by the Luftwaffe. Even more inconveniently for the quisling *and* for Getz, he was in the building at the time and was killed; In the basement of the house there was a small trapdoor below which, was hidden some important papers that had survived the bombing and could incriminate certain of Herman's group members that still resided in Great Britain and were still active Nazis. Those papers were supposed to have been destroyed when Germany was defeated. It was believed that his Brenton operator had kept the documents for the purpose of blackmail.

Getz had been back and forth to the UK many times since the end of the war, clearing up loose ends as it were. If still in existence, He had to recover those papers. This was by far one of his most important assignments to date; His problem was, that up until recently he had no idea where they might be located. Although he had visited the bomb-site several times, Getz couldn't find what he was looking for. He was unaware of the existence of the trapdoor in the basement.

The Nazi got lucky. He found out about the trapdoor by means of an overheard conversation whilst he was doing some odd jobs, posing as Posh, in a local pub; It seemed that a local Police Constable had been slightly injured whilst chasing a couple of young boys off the bomb-site. Apparently, the bobby had fallen into the basement where the kids had been playing moments before. The incident was a great source of amusement to the locals, as the bobby that took the tumble was non too popular. The boys that were chased were two well known scallywags. The Constable was known as Tiny Joyce. The boys were Jimmy Green and Peter Brown. Getz had made a mental note of those names. Getz was completely unaware that the authorities, by means of good police work by Constable Joyce, were now in possession of the documents and had discovered his true identity. He had been at the top of the most wanted list for a long time. However, nobody had ever seen the man or could ever pinpoint his whereabouts. The authorities did know however, that the Nazi was very clever, resourceful, sometimes armed and always dangerous! A trap had been set for him.

'German, bloody German! That's what that accent was! No wonder he was asking all them bleedin questions! Who would-a-thought Posh was a bleedin German!' Pete's hoarse whispering sounded overly loud.

Jim put a finger to his mouth and hissed impatiently, 'shush ya noisy sod!'

After listening for awhile longer and concluding that there wasn't much more of interest to be heard, Jim indicated with a nod towards the road that it was time to move on. Pete acknowledged with a nod of his own. Carefully and quietly, the boys turned to leave. They froze to the spot when they saw the Nun barring their way!

She was very tall and very thin. Her stance was threatening. She had her hands on her hips as if she were carrying two rolls of imaginary lino. She glowered down at the boys. The look on her long gaunt face would have caused Big-Ben to miss a strike or two!

'And what are you two little scruffs up to? Mischief, of that I have no doubt!' She said slowly and in a reedy, menacing voice.

Not being of the catholic faith, neither Pete nor Jim had ever had occasion to speak to a Nun. Also, they had made it an unwritten rule that they should do all in their power to avoid getting this close to one. With the rule being unwittingly broken, the lads were, at that moment in time, at a loss as to what to say or do. Jim looked into the eyes of the formidable, black and white robed Nun. His dark features were set in the most defiant he could muster. No contest! Her solid, stony glare perished Jims' forced boldness. He looked down at the ground for a stone to push about with his foot. Pete was staring at Jim so that he didn't have to look at the Nun.

'Well, are you going to answer me?' Demanded the Nun sharply.

Pete drew in a deep breath and looked at the Nun, avoiding eye contact. He cleared his drying throat and managed to mumble an answer. 'Well, I; that is *we,* was on our way to the library Mrs, Miss, I mean Madam.' Not knowing how to address the Nun caused Pete to blush bright red. Neither of the lads noticed the corners of the Nuns' mouth turn up giving the hint of a smile.

'The Library does not open on Sundays boy.' She stated accusingly.'

'Ohhh, don't it?' Said Pete, pathetically trying to sound innocent.

'Oh shit.' murmured Jim softly, stupidly believing he wouldn't be heard.

'I heard that boy!' rasped the fearsome Lady. 'And. you are a liar!' she continued, angrily pointing a long, bony finger at Pete. Her wide, thin mouth was no longer showing any sign of a smile.

'Sorry; ever so sorry Miss.' Pete's stumbling apology was almost fawning.

The Nun sighed deeply and proceeded to preached an earnest warning at the boys. 'It is a mortal sin to tell lies, especially to a Nun or any other member of the Church. If you continue to lie to people, mark my words you will surely burn in Hell! Now, get away from here and stay away!'

Pete and Jim needed no more coaxing. They were up on their toes and away up the driveway in the blink of an eye! Once they were far enough away from the Nun, they slowed to walking pace. 'Sod that for a bleedin lark, she's more scary than me Aunty Bet!' Exclaimed Pete. It was rumoured that Aunt Bet had once killed a rent man!

'Yeah! 'I'd sooner av a run in with Tiny Joyce than one-o-them Nuns any-time and that's no lie!' Agreed Jim.

The lads walked hastily on towards the Library in silence. They passed by some more shops, the Fire and Ambulance Station and two sets of maisonettes, one on either side of the road. They had been built to a similar design as the ones the lads lived in. A high, brown-brick wall enclosing a small estate of private, expensive houses curved round the long bend in the road. There were a few more people out and about now. Some walking their dog. Some being walked by their dog; When the boys reached the crown of the curve they stopped. They stared in absolute amazement at the Library, or what was happening in and around the place. There were Police officers everywhere and some of them were carrying guns!

The library was a wide, single storey building constructed in the maner of a large, Mediteranean villa. It was built from a mixture of standard red brick and heavy, white masonry. Eight, large, white-stone framed windows were separated in the middle of the buildings' façade by a porch, the low, apex roof of which, was supported by two white-stone columns. Large, half glazed, double Oak doors served as the entrance to the library. The doors were wide open. A set of wide, concrete steps gave access to the porch. There were gardens fronting the building. Neatly kept flower beds and shaped patches of lawn grass were disected by a tarmac pathway leading from the pavement to the library steps. A long, low wall separated the gardens from the pavement. Clumps of evergreen shrubs grew in regular intervals along the length of the wall. The ornate, wrought iron gates to the place were missing. They were among the many such metal items sacrificed for the war effort.

A narrow tree and fence lined slip- road leading to the canal ran past the left side of the Library. This gave access to the rear of the building and the bomb site. To the rear of this was a high, barb wire topped wall enclosing a coach building yard and factory. The wall showed little sign of being damaged by the bombing. To the right of the library there stood the solid, grey-stoned and formidable looking Bank building.

There were three squad cars and a black Police van parked on the road in front of the Library. As the lads watched, a small lorry pulled up at the head of the canal road. Four Constables began hurriedly unloading it. They were unloading trestles and red and white, painted poles. The paraphernalia required to erect road blocks. Minutes later, the road-blocks were set. In front of each one stood a warning sign reading in large letters, POLICE STOP!

One road block was set up across the canal slip-road, another two across the main road denying access to within thirty yards of either end of the Library. One was only yards from where Jim and Pete were excitedly watching the urgent action. A Policeman was left guarding each road block. The one guarding the barrier close to the boys, eyed the two suspiciously. It was none other than Tiny Joyce. People were beginning to gather at the barriers. They looked puzzled, bemused. They were quietly chattering among each other and questioning the Constable. Tiny kept droning the same sentences 'Keep well back folks. We have a seige situation. There's an armed man on the bomb site. We have the area completely surrounded.'

Pete and Jim watched as the Police positioned themselves around the site, pistols at the ready. They couldn't see all of the site as more than half was obscured from them by the Library building. They didn't need to see the whole area though, as they knew the layout well, they had spent a lot of time playing around the place in the past. They knew of plenty of places for the coppers to get cover behind. Half demolished walls and out-buildings. Piles of rubble, sewer trenches, storm drains etc; Pete and Jim looked at each other. They both had the same thought in their mind. They wished they could get closer.

'Blimey Pete, av you ever seen anything like this?' Jims' voice was pitched high, he was almost choking with excitement.

'Course I aint, you know I aint ya daft sod!' Pete sounded equally manic.

'Come on, lets get to the barrier!' Jim urged.

They made their way to the end of the barrier that was closest to the action. Most of the other onlookers were gathered there. It was still fairly early on a Sunday morning but the small group of people was growing in number and a few cars had pulled up and parked along the kerbside. Jim and Pete managed to edge their way to the cross-bar of the barrier. They surveyed the scene. Jim gave Pete a nudge and with a gesture of his head he drew Petes' attention to the site of some road-works that were about fifteen yards inside the barrier and closer to the bombsite. The road-works consisted of a shallow trench and a watch-mans hut surrounded by a light-weight barrier. Pete looked from Jim to the roadworks and then back to Jim again. He was shaking his head slowly from side to side. He had a horrified expression on his face and was silently mouthing the words, no, no, no. Jim looked disappointed; The boys were quiet but tense. They scanned the scene intently. They were so keyed up and expectant they couldn't keep still; They froze when the sharp crack of a gunshot rang out!

Instinctively, everybody ducked, some backed away from the barrier, a woman shrieked. Seconds later, two more shots were fired, then all Hell broke loose! The racket of many weapons being fired filled the air! The occasional whining of ricochets added to the cacophony! Jim and Pete whooped with excitement!

'I thought the bloody war was over!' Shouted a man in the crowd.

'Me too!' Called another.

'Keep low, keep low!' Shouted the Constable.

As abruptly as the shooting started, it stopped! Less than thirty seconds had passed between the first shot and the last; In the relative silence Pete and Jim could hear each others excited breathing. They glanced at one another, their eyes shining and smiling broadly. Orders to hold firing were barked through a loud hailer at the small army of Police Officers. Moments later another car arrived and parked at the kerbside. The car had brought a reporter and a photographer from the local newspaper. When the reporter enquired as to what was going on, every body in the crowd tried to give their version of events at the same time. The photographer tried to duck under the barrier. Tiny stopped him in his tracks and told him in no uncertain terms to keep back. Jim and Pete never took their eyes off the siege scene, they were afraid to blink for fear of missing something; Pete's attention was drawn to some activity at the library entrance; He could hardly believe what he was seeing!

There was one Police Officer left guarding the main entrance to the Library. He was unarmed and he was being held at gunpoint by the Nazi Getz! Somehow Getz had found a way to get into the Library from his hide-out! There must have been a hidden tunnel. It was obvious by their lack of urgency that the Police surrounding the bomb-site were unaware of his escape from their trap! Pete grabbed Jims' arm and pointed at the scene. Jim gasped at the sight. They both glanced at Tiny, he was looking in completely the wrong direction! Getz was talking to his captive but due to distance and the noise of the crowd, his words were barely audible. Getz raised his pistol higher, pointing it at the Constables head! The captive had his arms spread wide and was talking back at Getz. He seemed to be trying to persuade him to give it up! A shot was fired! The Policeman's helmet flew up and away! The Constable crumpled to the ground like a discarded overcoat!. Jim and Pete watched in shocked, horrified disbelief!

At the sound of the shot, gasps and uttered curses rippled through the startled crowd. When Constable Joyce saw what had happened to his colleague, he yelled, almost screaming at Getz! 'YOU MURDERING BASTARD, YOU MURDERING NAZI BASTARD!' Getz fired a shot at the enraged Policeman! Miraculously, the bullet not only missed the Officer, it missed everybody in the crowd! It slammed noisily into the wind-screen of the reporters car shattering it! Pandemonium ensued!

The onlookers scattered in all directions! Getz, with murderous determination set hard in his features, ran headlong across the library gardens towards the line of squad cars! He tripped and fell. He came up running and shooting in all directions. He was splattered with mud. Half a dozen or so of the Police from the bombsite were running, keeping low, along the side of the Library! Although unarmed, Tiny was purposefully striding, his big fists clenched and poised, towards the library entrance. His features were set in determined vengeance! Several shots were fired by the Police! The order to hold your fire was shouted! Getz dove into one of the cars! He started it up and with tyres screeching and smoking, he drove the two-ton squad car straight at the striding Policeman and the barrier beyond! The courageous but foolhardy copper stopped in his tracks and stood his ground. The car's engine was screaming! Getz had his foot hard down! His knuckles shone white on either side of the steering wheel! His face was set solid and grey in a blend of fear and hatred!

The order to open fire at the speeding car was screamed out! Pete and Jim were fozen to the spot behind the barrier tressle! They watched in terrified fascination as bullet after bullet struck the car! Tiny at last saw sense and dived for cover! The sound of tyres bursting and shredding and shattering glass only added to the racket of the tortured, screaming engine! The sharp crackle of gunfire and the heavy calibre bullets slamming into, or ricocheting off the speeding car was ear-splitting!

More by luck than by judgement, Getz got hit! The round hit him in the right cheek-bone shattering it. The bullet passed through behind his nose, hit the inside of his left cheek-bone, turned downwards and exited, in a gout of blood, through his lower jaw. Getz slumped to his right dragging the steering wheel down as he went. The bullet riddled squad car lurched violently to the right, smashed through the barrier around the small road-works and with the din of twisting, crushing metal, nose-dived into the trench sending a shower of dirt and stones into the air.

After the frantic, horrific happenings, the relative quiet seemed somehow unreal. It was as though the doors of hell had been slammed shut; Jim and Pete watched breathlessly as a cloud of smoke and steam rose slowly from under the car bonnet. They were both shaking a little. A mixture of emotions confused them, fear, horror, excitement and elation were some of them. They got slowly to their feet staring at the wreckage. They were still unable to fully comprehend what they had just witnessed. Jim was the first to speak.

'Bloody Hell!' He stated simply and evenly.

'Keep well back boys!' ordered Tiny as he cautiously moved towards the wreck.

The boys threw a quick glance in his direction, nodded and then returned to a crouching position. They almost jumped out of their skin when the front, nearside car door flew open slamming into Tiny, knocking him backwards and over onto his back! He landed badly, he yelped in agony! Getz had kicked the door open and was emerging from the smoking wreck! The boys stood up and stepped back several steps as they watched in horror as Getz dragged himself out of the car and got shakily to his feet! His face was a repulsive mask of blood and filth! Bubbles of blood and mucus grew and burst from his smashed nose and mouth as he breathed! His shattered jaw oozed thickening blood and fragments of teeth and bone! The shoulders and front of his jacket were soaked in blood! His left arm hung twisted at his side, it was broken in several places! His right hand moved towards the pistol that was tucked into his belt! Pete grabbed frantically at Jims' left arm with both hands pulling him and yelling 'RUN JIM, RUN FOR IT FOR CHRISTS SAKE!' To Pete's utter disbelief Jim grabbed his hands, wrenched them off his arm and shoved him violently away! The look in Jims' eyes shocked Pete; It was the look of a madman!

The horrifying form of Getz staggered and stumbled towards Jim. Although he couldn't see the Germans eyes for thick gore, the boy felt the malevolence emitting from them! He could feel hatred boring into him! He could hear people shouting at him but the voices seemed to come from a thousand miles away. He watched the big, bloodied hand of the Nazi closing round the grip of the pistol; Without taking his eyes off of Getz his knees bent as he went down and grabbed up the pebble that was laying between his feet. In one smoothe, well practiced move he straightened up, balanced himself, drew back his right arm, stretched his left straight out in front and hurled the stone full pelt at Getz!

The sound of the near perfectly formed pebble hitting skull-bone sounded sickeningly loud. The Pebble struck home on Getz's forehead, just above the bridge of the nose. The tall Nazi gasped and halted his murderous advance. Getz forgot about the pistol as he tried to raise his quivering hand to his head. The hand only got chest high before he dropped to his knees with an agonized groan. His whole body shuddered. He swayed back and forth for a few moments, then he slumped forward and fell with a dull thud onto his bloody, ruined face.

Happily, the shot Policeman survived the cold-blooded shooting. It later emerged that the pistol, a German luger, had been loaded with a mixture of good amunition and duds. For some obscure reason, some of the bullets were slightly smaller than was practical for use in the German pistol? Luckily for the Constable, he was shot with such a bullet. The velocity of the bullet was not enough to do nearly as much damage as would a proper round; The gallant copper was left blinded in one eye and with some scarring to his head and face. He was more than thankful however, to have come out of the dreadful ordeal with his life and a decoration awarded by the Home Secretary for his outstanding courage.

Herman Getz survived the gunshots, the car-crash and the stone that felled him. His unconscious body was whisked rapidly away from the scene of the incident to a secret place to recover from his injuries. Upon recovering, he was sent back to Germany in exchange for a British national that had been held in a German prison for several years. Herman Getz was never heard of, or from again.

Peter Brown was left in a state of mild shock after witnessing the the sequence of horrific and frightening events that had occurred at the roadblock. With the loving care of his parents and some prescribed medication, the boy was back to normal in a matter of weeks; Sadly, this was not the case for Jimmy Green. Fearing his Fathers' wrath, when the lad got home, he said nothing to anybody in his family about what he had been involved in during that initially exciting, but ultimately terrifying mornings events. He lived in fear of his Father finding out for some time. Very little of the events were published in the Newspapers. This was due to the Home Office, for reasons known only to themselves, suppressing the story. It was inevitable though, that Jims' parents would find out, via the grapevine, about their son's involvement in the incident.

Due to a combination of a mass of bottled up emotions and the severe beating he received, Jimmy Green changed from being a normal fun loving, mischievous boy to a withdrawn, morose and often, violent boy. It was for those reasons that, through time Pete and Jim, saw less and less of one and other until it came to the point of doing little more than nod to each other in passing. Truth be told, Pete became too afraid to be around his once, best pal.

In the fullness of time, Pete made a good life for himself. Through hard work and determination he managed to get a place in university and went on to become a successful Lawyer.

Sadly, things didn't work out so well for Jim. He became a loner. He withdrew deeper into himself. He became more and more depressed; It was later discovered that he had suffered increasingly more severe, physical and mental cruelty at the hands of his deranged Father over a long period of time; After leaving school, Jim drifted in and out of work for a couple of years. Almost inevitably he met up with and became friendly with some youths that were often in trouble with the law. It wasn't long before Jim himself was convicted of a crime of violence. His reputation as a 'hard man,' as it were, grew to the extent that he was feared by many of the residents of Brenton.

Tiny Joyce however, was *not* afraid of Jimmy Green. It was rumoured that Tiny, whilst walking his beat one evening, bumped into Jim and they had a 'bit of a chat,' so to speak. As a consequence of that meeting, Jim joined the Army; Naturally, this changed his life. He was directed, Army style, back on to the straight and narrow; Jimmy Green served his country with honour and bravery as an Infantry soldier in the Korean War; He never returned from the conflict.

END

Rat Trap!

Rat trap tells of the story of a lonely old Man and his sick obsession with the killing of Rats!

He holds down a part time job as a night watchman. Being a pensioner, he needs the extra income. The old Man had spent most of his working life as a Mariner and had a vast experience of life, the World and people. He had never married and had no living relatives. All he had were lots of memories, good and bad.

This short tale tells of one of those memories, a bad one. It was more than just a memory though. It was a horrific nightmare, a nightmare that would recur often and plague the old Man for most of his adult life. The nightmare began for him after a terrible incident that occurred when he was a young boy. An accident resulted in the death of his best friend. If that were not enough, a further incident involving himself and his deceased pal led to the old Man developing an a hatred of rats which, after a while became an unhealthy obsession with the mutilating and killing of the said creatures; The conseouences of his actions were, to say the least, dire!

This is a very dark and perhaps to some, scary story.

ENJOY!

Rat Trap!

The night watchman was sitting hunched over in a stained threadbare, old armchair. He had recently returned from his first patrol of the night. The premises he was looking after was once a rope manufactuing complex. Long disused, the once thriving site and buildings were now derelict, and dangerous to be near. In the winter months the site was mostly a slippery lake of mud. In the dry summers it was a choking dustbowl. The site was like a small ghost town and unless, like the night watchman, you knew your way around the place, you could easily get hurt and it maybe be some time before you could expect to get help, if any at all.

There was little risk of anybody breaking on to the site, for it was common knowledge to the local petty thieves and totters that the site had long since been stripped of every thing that was of any value. Also, the local vandals steered clear of the place. It had a certain reputation and was known to be rat infested. In the past, there had been several attempts to rid the area of vermin but none seemed to have had much of an effect upon the rat population. Even the feral cats kept clear of certain areas of the site.

Old Jim, the night watchman, was employed merely to keep insurance costs to a minimum for the owner of the site. Jim didn't like the job much, however, it suited him in as much as he was his own boss and the meagre wage he received helped supplement his even more frugal pension. He was a loner, almost a recluse. He preferred his own company and would only speak when spoken to for the sake of good manners. He was a tall, thin, haggard looking man. His features were dark and swarthy. A shock of iron-grey hair topped his wide forehead. Dark, bushy eyebrows drooped over deep set, brown eyes. His broken nose was hooked to one side; his mouth was wide and cruelly thin. The old mans' appearance made him look fierce and unfriendly, so people tended to keep their distance. That was how he liked it. He had long been of the opinion that relationships of any kind made life complicated. He had a rather cynical philosophy. The more friends a man has, the more enemies he is likely to make.

Jim still had on his heavy, well worn, Navy watch coat and his thick woollen scarf. It was mid November and it was cold and damp inside the musty old hut that served as his mess room. The hut was situated at the foot of an incline close to the centre of the site. It was surrounded with empty crates, large cable reels and other rotting junk. It had originally been used as a paint store. The odour of paint had long since dissipated. Now, the only smells were those of dampness, mice droppings and general decay. The hut was little more than a sixteen souare foot, wooden box. The apex roof was steep and there was no ceiling. Some of the rafters and joists were covered with mildew and were slowly rotting away. The floorboards were creaky and rotten in places and were marked with numerous faded, congealed paint stains.

The only source of heating in the hut was a small pot bellied stove in front of which, Jim was sitting huddled up, trying to get warm. The only furniture in the place, apart from the armchair, was a small side table and a cupboard that was fastened to the wall next to the only doorway. On top of the cupboard there was a selection of battered old pots and pans. There were no windows. They had long since been solidly boarded up. The only sounds in the dim, draughty structure were those of the comforting sound of the kettle coming to the boil and the spitting and crackling of coal burning in the stove.

Outside, a blanket of freezing fog was rapidly enveloping the old 'ropery' and the sites on either side of the nearby river. The icy mist already obscured the river. Only the sound of groaning, straining ropes indicated the presence of vessels at their moorings. The lonely sound of foghorns could be heard as they sounded out their warnings from the buoys and the ships at anchor, a mile or so off shore.

Jim rose from the armchair as the water in the kettle approached boiling point. He wrapped a cloth around his hand, took the kettle from off the stove and brewed a pot of strong tea. After leaving it stand for a minute or two, he filled his chipped and stained, pint-sized mug with the steaming brew and returned to the comfort of his chair. Sipping his tea, he stared up at the darkness above the decaying rafters. There was only one dingy, low wattage light bulb hanging from a long, twisted length of fraying wire lighting the hut, or trying to light the hut. Jim felt a little uneasy. He had felt that way since he walked through the gates of the site to start his shift. The site was unusually quiet. He couldn't put his finger on it, but he felt that something wasn't quite right. Earlier, whilst on patrol, he hadn't encountered or even seen a single feral cat, of which there were ouite a lot living on the site. Even the feral pigeons that occupied some of the site buildings were quiet. There were however, plenty of rats in evidence. More than usual, he thought. He dismissed the thought with a loud slurp of his tea and murmured with a chuckle, 'your imagining things you silly old fool.'

The old man pulled the collar of his coat high up around his ears. He encompassed the mug with both of his gnarly, bony hands. He relaxed back in the armchair and began pondering. His train of thought followed a pattern that rarely varied. He would think of what he had done during the day and would try to think of something difterent to do tomorrow. He never could. Inevitably, his thoughts would drift backwards to his past. He would think longingly of the oceans and seas he had sailed and of the many foreign lands he had visited. He would try to remember the many people he had met but rarely got to know. He tried to fit names to faces, faces to names but never quite managed to get them right. He thought of the good times he had known, but as always, his recollections would be haunted by memories of bad times, of which there were many. At that point, he would break the train of thought before he became morose.

The temperature was falling. A shiver shook his body. He put his near empty mug down and leaned forward to stoke up the stove. He grabbed the door hook-come poker from the hearth. Suddenly, he stopped what he was doing and listened intently.

'Something's up', he whispered softly. The silence in the hut was almost total. The coal in the stove no longer crackled, it had been reduced to embers. Nothing stirred; 'Mice! He rasped loudly, there aint no mice!' Although not over run, there were always a few mice scurrying about in the shadowy corners of the hut. It was most unusual not to hear them especially on the colder nights. Jim didn't mind the mice; sometimes he would even give them a crumb or two of his sandwiches, that is, if he had bothered to bring any with him. Perhaps the cats have got 'em all, he though doubtfully.

Pushing the thoughts of cats and mice from his mind, Jim continued with the the task of stoking up the stove. The racket of the shovel and the coalscuttle sounded over-loud in the gloomy confines of the hut. On completion of the stoking up, he went to the cupboard and took out a three ouarters empty bottle of South African brandy and a grubby glass. On closing the cupboard door, several flakes of dull, green paint fluttered to the floor. 'Bloody place is falling to bits,' he muttered. Once back in his chair, he pulled it a little closer to the stove and poured himself a liberal tot of the cheap booze declaring loudly, 'you cant beat a drop of good old rocket fuel!' He then took out from his faded, navy blue waistcoat his dented and scratched pocket watch. Peering at the dark hands on the grey face he muttered, 'I'll give it another half an hour or so and I'll have another walk round the site'. At that, he relaxed back and sipped at his drink.

The old man listened to the comforting sound of the replenished stove popping and crackling as the fire slowly worked to consume the damp coal. For the first time that night he began to feel the benefit of the stove. The combination of the warmth and the effect of the brandy began to take its toll. His eyes became leaden; his mind was almost empty of thought. He began to doze. Suddenly, a loud 'SNAP!' jerked the night watchman from his stupor. It was the noise of one of the many traps that he had set strategically around the hut. A trap had been triggered and Jims' traps were usually deadly. The old man hissed cruelly through bared, yellow teeth. 'Gotcha you filthy vermin!' His eyes glistened in their deep, dark sockets and his mouth was set in a wicked grin. He reached into the inside pocket of his coat and took out a dog-eared notebook. A stub of pencil doubled as a bookmark. Opening the book, he drew a short vertical line on the page. There were many of these marks in the book. In fact, there were hundreds. The marks were neatly arranged in blocks of five. Each single mark represented the demise of a rat.

It could be said that the old night watchman had an obsession with rats, that is to say, the killing of them. He vehemently hated them. He had despised rats for as long as he could remember. People that actually like rats are few and far between. Some people are able to tolerate them however, if the truth is known, most people hate and fear the verminous creatures. Jim was afraid of rats; he had good reason to be.

Many years in his past, when he was eight years old, he was witness to a terrible and tragic accident. It happened on a beautiful July morning. He and his friend were hanging about around their favourite playground, the canal that ran close by to where they lived. Like most children of their age, water, except for the stuff they had to wash in, was an almost irresistible attraction. On this particular occasion, it became a fatal attraction. Jims' best friend Paul fell into the canal. He couldn't have fallen in at a worse, more dangerous place. He fell in close to a set of lock gates on the lower reach side and the sluices were open, turning the water beneath them into a foaming, thundering, watery, death trap. Young Jim never saw his friend go into the water; he was busy studying the skeleton of a bird that was lying under an elderberry tree. He was contemplating on how the unfortunate bird had met its end. He never heard Paul cry out either, the noise of the sluices would drown out any noise Paul would have made. The first that Jim knew of what had happened was when he saw the lock keeper franctically winding the heavy, iron handle trying to close the sluices.

Young Jim ran to the edge of the canal below the gates. The lock keepers voice could only just be heard over the din of rushing water as he screamed at Jim to get back from the edge. At that moment, Jim spotted Paul's brightly clothed body pitching and rolling in the tumultuous, muddy brown water. Jim was frozen to the spot as he watched his friend disappear from sight. He began screaming out Paul's name against the roar of the rushing water. Moments later, to his horror, he saw the ginger haired, freckly Paul rising in the filthy canal. The face was not that of his friend. It was a mask from hell, frozen in pain and terror. It was as white as chalk. The mouth was wide open, as were the eyes and they stared up at Jim as if pleading to him for help. He took a step closer to the edge. The mask disappeared; it was sucked hack into the maelstrom. Jim leaned forward to jump. A large, strong hand grabbed his shaking shoulder. 'Don't be silly lad leave it to us!' Jim turned and looked up at the policeman and said simply, stupidly, 'he's my friend and we must get home for our dinner.'

After what seemed an age to young Jim, but was no more than minutes, the noise of rushing water slowly diminished as the sluice gates were finally shut. Another bobby joined the one that had restrained him. Stripped to the waist, they took it in turns to dive into the murky water to try and find Paul. Suddenly, a woman rushed past Jim, almost knocking him over. She screamed, 'Paul! Paul!' as she jumped into the canal. Her dress billowed in the water as she blindly splashed and floundered about. Jim looked on in numbed, horrified silence as the policemen fought to get Paul's struggling, sobbing Mother out of the water. Jim hoped upon hope but he knew in his heart of hearts that his friend was lost. Time and time again, the policemen duck dived, but their efforts were in vain. A crowd of people had gathered at the canals edge, Jim could no longer see what was going on. He turned away and headed for home. He was in silent, dazed shock. He couldn't believe that he would never see his friend again. His bitter, anguished tears did not come until he was in the quiet privacy of his bedroom.

Despite exhaustive searches, it was five days before Paul's body was found. The discovery was purely by chance, and the fickle hand of fate played the worst trick possible on young Jim, for it was he that found the body of his friend, or what was left of it.

It was a bright, clear afternoon. Jim was alone. He was skimming stones across a weir that ran off the canal about a mile from where Paul had lost his life. It was a pleasant, grassy spot surrounded by low shrubs and trees. It was one of Jims' favourite parts of the canal. Despite being warned to stay away from the place, he felt that it was his duty to continue to hang about the 'cut'.

He reckoned that Paul would like him to keep visiting their favourite haunts. He was however, reluctant to go near the lock gates.

Naturally, Jim was thinking about his friend. He was thinking how much better at skimming stones Paul was than himself when suddenly, a large, brown rat ran in front of him, almost over his shoes! Instinctively, Jim jumped back. He was startled but not scared, he was used to seeing rats in the vicinity of the canal. His eyes followed the path of the creature. It stopped in its' tracks about twenty yards from him, raised itself onto its' haunches and sniffed the air. Slowly, Jim bent down and picked up a hefty stone. The rat showed signs of moving on, so without taking aim, Jim threw the stone hard at the brazen rodent. The missile missed by a good margin. It bounced high off the springy, mossy grass and over some shrubs that were growing beside the weir 'bottoms.' The stone landed with an audible, muddy 'plop' behind the densely leaved shrubbery. Instantly, at least a dozen rats dashed out from behind the shrubs and scattered in all directions, one of them ran between Jims' legs. 'Blimey!' He gasped; He was taken aback at seeing so many rats at one time.

Slowly, nervously he walked towards the bushes. An awful stench filled the motionless, warm air causing him to gag. Hundreds of fat blowflies buzzed around the area just behind and above the shrubs. Gingerly, he kept moving forward, despite the sick feeling of dread in his stomach. On reaching the chest high shrubs he looked down. The sight that met young Jims' gaze was the source of a horrendous nightmare that would recur for the rest of his life. His whole body stiffened on recognition of his lost friends' clothes, half immersed in a swamp of stinking muck. Despite being shredded and smeared with oily, black mud and slime, the bright colours could still be seen. Jim stared; his eyes wide with disbelief at the repulsive sight that lay before him in the stinking filth. What remained of the once, bright, cheerful Paul was beyond recognition.

The limbs of the corpse were twisted at un-natural, grotesoue angles. Paul's red unruly hair was matted with oily filth and bits of weed. It was plastered across his forehead, the skin of which was a dark, purple colour. There were chunks of the wrinkled flesh missing, exposing the bone of the skull. Bits of eyelids and eyebrows with tiny ginger hairs hung over black, empty eye sockets that seemed to stare into Jims' unblinking, watery eyes. There was a black, triangular hole where there was once a nose. Blackened cheekbones showed through shrivelled, blue-black shreds of rotting flesh. The uneven teeth protruded starkly from a lipless mouth, mettle fillings glinted in the sunlight. Little remained of the gnawed flesh of the lower jawbone and the ears were all but eaten away.

The boy stood motionless, petrified, as he stared down at the ghastly death mask. He was entranced. His shocked, frantic mind was trying to reconstruct the bright, cheerful features of his pal, to put the ruined features into some kind of order. The repeated efforts were in vain. His trance like state was broken when his attention was drawn to a movement lower down on the putrid remains. A large rat had become trapped inside the fleshless, empty chest cavity. A piece of driftwood was lodged in the gaping, oozing hole where the stomach once was. Unable to escape, the panicked rat desperately gnawed at the rib bones. Its' long, yellow, chisel like teeth chewed and tugged at the human cage. The disgusting beast was covered in black slime and shreds of rotting flesh.

Jim opened his mouth wide in a bid to scream, to release the mad, grisly confusion that filled his his mind and to rid his nose and mouth of the stink and the foul, bitter taste of death. The only sounds he could manage were choking and gurgling noises. He took several unsteady steps backwards and with his mouth still agape he began to shake violently, uncontrollably. When the scream finally came, it was long and shrill. His staring, glazed eyes released the tears. They coursed down his ashen cheeks and dripped from his ouivering chin. He screamed himself hoarse. He stood sobbing for some minutes. Each heaving sob shook him to his feet. Then, suddenly; he was calm. It was as if he'd been slapped in the face. He stood motionless for several minutes, glanced up at the sky, turned about and walked away from the nightmarish scene.

Although Jims' parents were aware of the fact that a friend of their son had drowned, they were unaware that the boy was a close friend and that Jim had actually witnessed the tragedy, also, that it was he that discovered the remains of the unfortunate boy several days later. Jim couldn't bring himself to report the gruesome discovery to the authorities. He did not want anybodyto see his pal in such an awful state. Paul's remains were not found 'offically' for two more days.

Jim's parents were baffled by the extraordinary change in their son's personality. Whereas once, he was a happy go lucky, somewhat mischievous lad, he had become withdrawn and morose. His sleepless, troubled nights worried his parents more than anything else. Try as they might, they could not get him to open up to them. Nobody ever found out the cause of the drastic change in Jims' persona. Although the nightmares became less frequent as Jim grew older, they would occur from time to time and would always follow the same pattern. He would see the skeleton of the bird. He would see the coloured clothing flashing as the body pitched and rolled. Then he would hear the shouts of the lock keeper. Then he would see the policemen pulling off their tunics, kicking off their boots and diving into the deadly canal. The dreadful nightmare always ended with the cheeky, cheerful face of Paul gradually changing into the horrific death mask, surrounded by bloated, slimy rats that appeared to be grinning at Jim, mocking him!

In the gloom of the damp, chilly hut, the night watchman sat quietly thinking. He made no move to go outside and check his traps, particularly the triggered one. He didn't feel the need. He had full confidence in the reliability of the deadly devices. They were of the best ouality and they were well maintained by the man himself. There was little chance of malfunction. In addition, old Jim had modified his traps. He did this by painstakingly filing down the 'snap bar' on each trap until they were razor sharp. The result being, when the trap was sprung, the rat would be decapitated, or at the very least, severely mutilated. If any other creature fell foul of the traps, although unfortunate, it was a price worth paying us far as Jim was concerned. So, he reckoned that there would be time enough to check his traps on his next patrol of the site. Yes indeed it could be said that the old man was obsessed with the killing of rats.

After replacing the record of rat killings in his coat pocket, Jim drank off the rest of the tot of brandy. He was about to give the stove a poking when he heard a faint, odd sound. He had spent many long nights on the site and was familiar with all the sights and sounds thereon. The sound he'd just heard was different, strange. It was a series of taps followed by scratching sounds. Gradually, the sounds increased in volume. Also, they sounded somehow, 'purposeful'. The sounds seemed to be coming from the foot of the wall behind the stove. Jim stood and bent to look behind the stove, it was dark down there, the weak light from the cheap light bulb failed to penetrate the dimness. Jim listened; the sound came again. It appeared to be coming from outside. Then, more scratching began on the opposite wall. The two sets of sounds seemed to be echoing one and other, like a repetitive signal. The sounds grew louder. Jim stepped to the middle of the hut. He glanced from side to side at the walls. He was perplexed, the sounds were beginning to annoy him! Abruptly, the sounds stopped. It was quiet in the hut once more.

Scratching his head the old man returned to his armchair. He was about to sit down when the weird noises started again, only this time they were coming from the roof and they were much, much louder! Jim froze as the two sets of what had become 'banging' and scratching, were joined by another set and then another and they kept coming until there were many. The noises were no longer like signals, there was no rhythm. Soon, the whole hut seemed to be vibrating with the cacophonous racket. Jim stared up at the rafters. His eardrums were ringing, he was getting annoyed and he was unnerved. He shouted at the top of his voice. 'GET OUT OF IT, GET AWAY FROM HERE!' The unearthly racket continued, even louder! Jim strode to the corner where the broom was kept, grabbed it up and returned to the middle of the hut. He hammered at the rafters with the broom shank as hard as he could. Chunks of damp dirt fell onto his head and shoulders. Some fell into his mouth, he spluttered and spat the muck out. 'GET THE HELL AWAY FROM ME!' He bellowed. For a moment it seemed that the noise was fading, but only for a moment. The clamour was soon building up again and it wasn't long until it was as loud as it was before! Suddenly, the din of the scratching doubled in volume. It sounded to Jim like barbed wire being dragged back and forth across the roof. The ear splitting racket was hellish! Instinctively, Jim released his grip on the broom, ducked down and covered his head with his hands.

He remained in that position until, to his great relief, the sound began to abate. Soon the hut was left in eerie silence. The moisture of his panting breath hung in the chilly air. Despite the cold, beads of sweat had formed on his brow. He raised his head and stared up into the rafters. Slowly, shakily he straightened up. He drew in a deep, shuddering breath and exhaled slowly, quietly. The sweat dried on his body and he began to shiver. Pulling his coat collar high up about his ears, he made his way back to the armchair; With trembling hands he took out his watch, then he put it away again. He wasn't really bothered about the time, because for the time being, he was more than a little reluctant to venture outside and investigate the cause of the frightening, uncanny noises, let alone patrol the site.

He sat back in the armchair. He tried to slow his rate of breathing. It seemed as if the whole hut was filled with the steam of his breath. Purposefully, he breathed slowly and deeply. After a while, he started to relax a little. He cast his mind back to the many times in his well-travelled life that he had been afraid. He had weathered those situations well because he knew who, or what it was that he was fearful of. What had occurred in the last few minutes was beyond his experience. Fear of the un-known was a new trial for Jim. 'What the hell was that all about?' He murmured softly. He fought to prevent his imagination from running riot. Dubiously, he came to the conclusion that the bizarre and frightening noises were due to an odd weather situation. In the silence, he peered around the dim, damp, shadowy hut and whispered hoarsely, 'at least I hope that's all it was'.

He picked up the poker again and with an act of bravado he poked the embers of the stove noisily. After adding a few more lumps of coal he listened quietly for a minute. Then he sniffed loudly and splashed the remains of the brandy into his glass and downed the fiery liquid in one gulp. He told himself that he should have gone outside to investigate. He felt ashamed of being afraid to; He could not recall a time when he was unable to confront his fear. He told himself it was nothing to be ashamed of; He failed to convince himself. Slowly, the brandy began to warm his insides and the warmth of the stove comforted the old man. The tension in his mind and body began to ease. He tried to push the recent events out of his mind. He closed his tired eyes.

Moments later, they snapped open again and Jim sat bolt upright! The hairs on the back of his neck bristled. There were more strange sounds. They were different from the last lot, but just as weird. These were scuffling and shuffling sounds. And they seemed to be coming from just outside the door. They sounded busy, urgent. It sounded as if something or things were digging. Jim was staggered and appalled when he heard low whispering. It sounded like somebody, or something, was plotting. His voice sounded dry and shaky when he murmured, 'oh Christ no, not more.' His heart was pounding as he sat rigidly and stared at the door through the gloom. The sounds stopped for an instant. Then, his heart missed several beats when he heard his words hissed back to him. 'Oh Christ no!' The voice sounded like it could have come from Satan himself. Fear gripped the old mans' heart like a steel claw. The temperuture in the hut plummeted!

Without warning, a thunderoud CRASH split the evil air! The hut shook violently. Something heavy had smashed into the outward opening door and almost drove it through its frame and into the hut! The meagre furniture jumped off the floor. Pots and pans clattered down from the cupboard. The brandy bottle and glass smashed down. Dirt and debris showered down from the crumbling rafters. Jim thought the hut was going to collapse. He dived for the corner behind him. To his horror, the quivering light bulb flashed brightly for an instant and then died. He crouched in the near, pitch darkness; His breathing was fast and jerky; Grey freezing mist wafted into the hut through splits in the door planks. The mist mingled with the condensation of his breath. He wretched violently when the atmosphere was filled with a ghastly, gut wrenching stench! The malevolent, guttural voice came a few seconds later. 'GOTCHA YOU FILTHY VERMIN!'

Absolute loathing was carried in the disembodied voice. It struck terror into the very soul of the old man. His chalk white face stood out manifestly in the freezing blackness. His trembling had nothing to do with the temperature. He swallowed hard several times. His mouth was dry and tasted foul. In a croaking, almost pleading voice he whispered, 'who's there? What do you want?' 'GOTCHA YOU FILTHY VERMIN!' The repeated words sounded even more baleful.

Panic was beginning to take hold. Jims' eyes darted in all directions. They strained as they tried to penetrate the darkness. The sound of his heavy breathing seemed to fill the claustrophobic blackness. He ached all over. Although he was afraid, he knew he had to move soon or before long, he wouldn't be able to move at all. Slowly, and as quietly as he could, he straightened his bony legs. With all his will he tried to regulate his breathing. He tried to calm down and gather his wits. He suddenly realised that the awful stink was now no more than a bad smell and that it didn't seem to be as cold in the wrecked hut. Panic eased its grip on the old man. He shivered in the dark silence and listened.

The loud metallic clattering of a frying pan skittering across the floor shattered the oppressive silence. Jims' heart almost stopped when it bounced off his foot. He gasped loudly and wretched, the disgusting stench was back! Abject terror gripped him when he heard the sound of low, wheezing breathing. His heart began palpitating when he felt the evil presence of someone, or something else in the hut. His whole body went rigid when the insidious presence emitted a low hissing snigger.

The old mans' bemused, fevered brain could take no more. His screaming words were almost incoherent. 'WHO ARE YOU? WHERE ARE YOU? WHAT THE HELL DO YOU WANT?' Then, totally overcome by panic, he lunged blindly in the direction of the doorway. He tripped and crashed headlong into the splintered door.

Blood streamed from gash in his forehead. He felt no pain. Franticly, he groped for the door-latch. His quivering fingers found it and yanked it up. The door would open no more than a couple of inches. Something was jamming it on the outside. He pushed and shoved with all his strength, it wouldn't budge. He shoulder charged it repeatedly until his shoulder was bruised and painful. He kicked and back healed the door, still it wouldn't give! He began sobbing pathetically. His desperation became even more manic. He screamed the screams of a madman as he hammered and punched the door. His blood smeared the flaking paint.

Soon, the rate and force of the blows dimished. Jims' strength was almost depleted. He begged the unyielding door to give way, to let him escape from the hellish trap. An emulsion of blood, sweat, dirt and tears masked his face. His hands were bruised and bloody. His shaking legs buckled and with his face pressed against the door, he slid slowly to his knees. His fingers clawed at the woodwork in a desperate attempt to stay on his feet.

The wretched night watchman sobbed pitifully. His shoulders heaved with each shuddering sob. He could feel no pain. His brain was numb. He was in a state of shock; After a while his sobbing abated as he drifted into unconsciousness, almost a coma. The hut was quiet again and the stink had gone. Nothing stirred except the gentle crackling and popping of the coal in the stove. Jim was slumped on the floor in the damp and the dirt. He was silent and motionless. He was so still, that if it wasn't for the vapour emitting from his drooling mouth, his stricken body could have been taken for dead. There was however, no peace for the old man. Soon, low, husky whispering sounds filled the hut. The scuffling noises began again. The whispering and scuffling sounds were interjected with malicious, evil sounding giggling.

Deep in the recesses of Jims' consciousness a sensation registered. Slowly, the sensation grew in strength. It became pain. His eyelids began to open and close rapidly; he was coming round. The pain grew in intensity. Then agony registered in his fevered brain as he realised that something was gnawing at his ankle! He jerked his leg out violently. There was more pain when the cold, stiff muscles of his thigh were wrenched. There was a loud squeal, the gnawing stopped.

Now that he was fully awake, the old mans' heart sank and filled with dark fear and dread. He realised that he had not awakened from an appalling, terrifying nightmare, a nightmare that was far worse than the recurring nightmare that had blighted his sleep for many years. This was a living nightmare. The hellish situation he was in now was real! For the first time in a long time, Jim began praying, fervently. He tried to raise his voice above the evil giggling. He couldn't, his throat was dry and painful.

The hoarse, mumbling prayers ceased abruptly. The night watchamn's heart leapt when he caught sight of an almost imperceptible glow of light. It wasn't much, but it was like a beacon to the man in the dark, lonely hell. A flicker of hope stirred in his heart. His gaze was locked on the feeble light. He dared not blink for fear of his beacon disappearing. Adrenalin began to kick in. It enabled him to struggle painfully to his feet. His right leg throbbed and pain stabbed at his ankle. Without taking his eyes off the dull, yellow glow, he leaned back on the bloody door. He pulled the collar of his filthy, bloodstained coat up around his ears. He clamped his hands firmly over his ears in an attempt to blot out the insufferable noises of scuffling and whispering. He stared at his beacon of hope.

His heart soared when he realised the light was getting brighter. He blinked his red rimmed, watering eyes for the first time in what seemed an age. 'Yes, yes, yes,' he hissed. The dirty yellow light bulb was coming back to life. The gloom was beginning to lift and Jims' feeling of hope grew stronger when to his joy, he realised that the unearthly noises that had plagued his ears and nerves had ceased. He began to believe whatever had been terrorising him had gone. As the glow of the bulb grew brighter and began penetrating the gloom, familiary began to take shape. The tatty old armchair. The stove and its' chimney. The table, now lying on its side. Pots and pans were gradually taking shape in the mist that swirled around the floor. Near the coalscuttle, the glass of the broken brandy bottle glimmered in the brightening light. A feeling of wonderful relief swept over the old man.

All feelings of wonderful relief were ripped from Jims' heart when the temperature in the hut plummeted and the nauseating stink filled the air yet again. Fear became his master again. Fear leapt to terror when he spotted an unfamiliar shape near the doorway. As the light grew brighter, Jim looked away from the dark, menacing shape. He didn't want to know what it was. Whatever it was, he knew it was evil; he could feel it in his heart, in his soul. Now, he no longer wanted the light to get any brighter. He didn't want to know what the shape was. Relentlessly, the light grew brighter. The shape began to take definite, terrible form. Some kind of unearthly influence forced Jim to turn his head towards the shape. He closed his tear filled eyes but, however hard he tried, he couldn't resist opening them.

The old man stared in horrified disbelief at the abomination that faced him. It was a monstrous RAT! The incredible, repulsive beast was sitting on its' haunches. It was three feet in height. Its' obese, pear shaped body was almost as wide. Its' fur shimmered in the yellow light, giving the satanic creature a ghostly aura. It was covered in stinking black slime and had shreds of putrefying flesh hanging from it. Jim's bulging, rheumy eyes stared into the inordinately large, amber eyes of the loathsome creature squatting six feet in front of him. The tiny black pupils were steady, piercing. They stared along its' long, tapered nose. The black nostrils flared and oozed greenish-yellow mucus that hung like a slimy beard. Just visible, behind the slime, were a pair of lethal looking, four inch long teeth. They looked like yellow chisels and were as sharp. They curved backwards under the creatures' lower mandible. Claws the size of eagles' talons protruded from grey, leathery feet. From behind its' bloated body, a long, black, serpentine tail laid across the floor. Silvery hairs bristled along its' quivering length. The abhorrent creature emiited the foul stench of death; On the floor, at the feet of the beast was Jims' record of rat killings! The detestable creature stared, unblinking. Its cruel hissing voice was laden with hatred. "GOTCHA YOU FILTHY VIRMIN!' The beasts satanic gaze penetrated to the depths of the old mans' soul. Unutterable terror dominated his quaking body.

Jim found himself staring down at his record book; After awhile he stopped shaking. Something 'clicked' in his mind. It was as if he had been slapped hard in the face. All feelings of dreadful terror drained from his mind and body. He knew his end was coming. He knew there was no escape from the vengeance of this creature from the depths of Hades. He felt cold. He felt so very, very tired. He took a last, long look around the shoddy old hut, his home from home. Then he turned his gaze on the creature that had put the fear of hell into him. He stared hard and steady, he was no longer afraid. Furious rage had replaced the fear.

A burst of adrenalin coursed through Jims' veins, as he was overwhelmed with unadulterated hatred. His eyes shone, his body shook. His lips peeled back revealing clenched teeth, he was grinning like a maniac. His large, bony hands were balled into tight, white-knuckled fists. He uttered in a low, croaking growl. 'Oh no, I've got you, you filthy vermin!' Then he lunged at the abomination. He didn't get far. The rats appeared from all around and in great numbers. They were all over him in seconds. He fought like a man possessed. He fought his last fight well and perhaps, with some relish, for he killed many of the murderous rodents. He crushed the life out of them with his bare hands. He threw them at the walls as hard as he could. He stamped them underfoot. He ripped them apart with his teeth. But the rats were too many. They were tenacious and crafty; they soon got into his clothes and the soft flesh beneath. Blood flowed from a thousand wounds. The night watchman's strength ebbed away as his life's blood pooled and mixed with the filth on the floor. He sank to his kneeds and emitted a long, sighing groan. He fell forward onto his face into the sticky, gory mess. He lay still for a few moments. The rats gorged. Then, with a mighty effort, Jim rolled over onto his back and flung his dripping arms out to the sides. He stared up wide-eyed, at the little yellow light bulb.

Jim felt a warm glow engulf his entire body, a feeling he hadn't felt for many a long year. As the rats began destroying his features, a red mist formed in his minds eye. The red mist slowly gave way to a pleasant, blue-white light. In the light, Jim could see the terrible death mask of his friend Paul. Mentally, Jim began to rebuild his friends' handsome young face. The wavy, red hair. The numerous freckles. The bright, sparkling blue eyes. The generous mouth; set in a cheeky grin. It was as if Paul could see Jim, for he winked and beckoned with his head. Then another face appeared in the vision. It was a dark, swarthy young face. It was young Jim himself. The smiling, faces looked down at the old night watchman. His wonderful vision and the pleasant light were slowly ushered away by the dark shroud of oblivion...

END